INTO A STRANGE LAND

INTO A STRANGE LAND

Unaccompanied Refugee Youth in America

Brent Ashabranner and

Melissa Ashabranner

Illustrated with photographs

DODD, MEAD & COMPANY

New York

Picture credits

Jeannine Daniels, pages 23, 24, 28, 29; UNHCR, pages 6–7, 10, 11, 15, 114, and 115.

1 2 3 4 5 6 7 8 9 10

Library of Congress Cataloging-in-Publication Data

Ashabranner, Brent K., date
   Into a strange land.

   Bibliography: p.
   Includes index.
   Summary: Presents individual stories of young
Southeast Asian refugees and discusses some of their
problems, hopes, and successes.
   1. Refugees—United States—Biography—Juvenile
literature.   2. Youth—United States—Biography—
Juvenile literature.   [1. Refugees]   I. Ashabranner,
Melissa.   II. Title.
HV640.4.U54A84   1987   362.8'7'0973   86-24357
ISBN 0-396-08841-4

Contents

For Jean-Keith Fagon

Acknowledgments

MANY PEOPLE helped us in gathering the material for this book. In addition to those persons mentioned in the text, we would like to thank Mark Franken, Migration and Refugee Services, United States Catholic Conference, Washington, D.C.; Nguyen Thi Viet Hang, Virginia L. Monteiro, and Andrew P. Reiss, Associated Catholic Charities, Washington, D.C.; Dennis Hunt, Karen Rosen, and Jill Wintersteen, Connections, Falls Church, Va.; Terry Kratovil, United Nations High Commissioner for Refugees, Washington, D.C.; Patricia King, Lutheran Social Services, Washington, D.C.; Lauren McMahon, Lutheran Immigration and Refugee Service, New York, N.Y.; Nancy Schulz, Children's Services, USSC, New York, N.Y.; Tsehaye Teferra, Ethiopian Community Development Council, Arlington, Va.; Monsignor Bryan Walsh, Catholic Community Services, Miami, Fla.; Thelma Ware, Social Services Office, Washington, D.C.

We are especially indebted to Loretta Tracy, director of the Associated Catholic Charities program for unaccompanied refugee minors in Tucson, Ariz., for insights that she gave us into all aspects of the program. We are grateful to Jeannine Daniels for use of her photographs taken when she was a UNHCR resettlement counselor in the Palawan Refugee Camp, Philippines. Other photographs in the book, except for those furnished by the UNHCR, were taken by Martha Ashabranner, Melissa Ashabranner, and Jennifer Ashabranner, who also printed them.

Brent Ashabranner
Melissa Ashabranner

INTO A STRANGE LAND

1 The Most Vulnerable People

T HE WAVES were not big now. Tran sat in the middle of the boat, crowded next to an old woman. She had put her arm around him during the night when the spray from the high waves was cold. He did not know her name. The boat was packed with people standing, sitting, a few lying down, but Tran could see no familiar face. Even now, on their third day at sea, he could not think clearly. He could not really believe what had happened. He knew he was not having a bad dream, but still he hoped he would wake up and be at his home in Vietnam.

The beginning had been good. Late in the afternoon, four days ago, Tran's father had told him they were going fishing, just the two of them. Tran was very happy because he had never been fishing with his father before. Tran's brother, who was ten and four years younger than Tran, cried because his father would not let him come. Tran remembered that his mother stood in the doorway of their house and watched them leave.

An hour later, when it was almost dark, Tran's father led them to a place on the beach where a man was waiting in a small boat. "Hurry," the man said. "You are late."

Tran and his father got into the boat, and the man poled them away from the shore. After awhile, Tran saw a big boat anchored in the bay. They headed toward it, and Tran saw other small boats going in the same direction.

"When are we going to fish?" Tran asked.

"Soon," his father said, "from the big boat."

Tran did not understand, but he said nothing more. Their boat came alongside the big boat; his father and the boatman grabbed a rope ladder from the big boat and pulled their own boat close. Tran's father handed Tran a small plastic bag.

"Climb up the ladder and do not lose the bag," he said.

Tran's eyes widened with fear. "No," he said. "I don't want to."

His father picked him up and swung him to the rope ladder. "I will follow," he said.

Then Tran climbed the ladder, gripping the bag tightly in one hand. When he reached the big boat's rail, two men waiting there swung him onto the deck. Tran saw that the deck was crowded with people. Most were men, but there were also women and children.

Tran looked down and saw that his father was still in the small boat. His father looked up at Tran and raised his hand. "Do not lose the bag," he said.

Then the boatman pushed the small boat away, and soon it was lost in the darkness. Tran cried out to his father, but one of the men standing beside him gripped him roughly by the shoulder. "Do not make noise," he said.

Tran clutched the boat's rail and stared into the night. His heart pounded. Perhaps his father had forgotten something and would return. But in only a few minutes the big boat's engine started up, and the boat moved quickly out to sea. Tran spun away from the rail and tried to run, but people were all around him, and he could hardly move. He held the plastic bag close, and he began to tremble.

After that, time ran together. During the dark night the boat began to roll, and Tran became seasick. He vomited until there was nothing in his stomach and then continued to retch until all the muscles of his body hurt. He lay on the deck and called for his mother. All around him people were sick; he could hear their moans over the noise of the boat's engine.

When at last the sun came up, the sea was calmer, and the boat did not roll so much. Tran was no longer sick, but he was terribly thirsty. He whispered for water, but no one heard him or paid any attention. Finally, a man came around with a bucket of water and gave everyone a single cupful. Tran drank his in a few gulps and then he was sick again. Sometime after that another man came around with a bucket of rice. He gave Tran a cupful, but Tran could not eat even one bite.

Now the sun overhead was hot and burned into Tran's skin. He cradled his head in his arms and slept all day on the deck. That night, when the waves came high again, he crawled to the middle of the boat and found a place beside the old woman.

It was not until the third day that Tran opened the plastic bag, although it had not been out of his hand, even for a moment. Some of his clothes were in the bag, and there was an envelope. He opened it and found a picture of his family that had been taken last year. He was in the picture with his mother and father, his two sisters, and his brother, Sinh.

A letter from his mother was also in the bag. The letter said she was sorry they could not tell him he was going away. She said the boat would take him to a refugee camp in a place called Thailand. She told him to tell the people who ran the camp that he wanted to go to America. She said she hoped someday the whole family could come or at least his brother when he was older.

Tran held the letter in his hand and stared at it. He knew about refugees. You could not live in Vietnam and not know about them. He had even thought that someday he might be a refugee, but had never imagined that he would leave Vietnam without his family.

Vietnamese refugees being rescued in the South China Sea.

Teen-age Vietnamese refugees.

"Are you alone?" the old woman asked.

For a moment Tran could not speak. At last he said, "I want to go home."

"Pray that we reach the refugee camp," the woman told him. "Do not even think about anything else."

Tran did reach a refugee camp in Thailand. He stayed there for a year before he was approved to enter the United States as a refugee. For two years now he has lived in New York with a foster mother and father who have two children of their own. Tran is in the tenth grade. He studies hard, especially English in a high-intensity language program, and is passing all his courses. He has his own room in his foster home. On the desk where he does his homework is the picture of his family in Vietnam, set in a small silver-colored frame which his foster parents bought for him. Tran tries hard to understand what has happened to him. He has written many letters to his mother and father, but he does not know if they have received them. He has received no answer, but he has not lost hope that someday a letter will come.

Since 1975, when the North Vietnamese completed their conquest of Vietnam, thousands of young refugees like Tran have come to America from the refugee camps of Southeast Asia. Smaller numbers have gone to England, France, Germany, Australia, and other countries. They arrive at the camps without their parents or other adult relative and—sometimes after months or even years of waiting— are brought to America or other countries to begin a new life.

Most of the "unaccompanied refugee minors," as they are called by the United States government, have come from Vietnam, but many have escaped from Cambodia and Laos. A growing number of young refugees are making their way from Ethiopia and Central American countries. About four out of five are teen-age boys, but many are teen-age girls and some are children no more than six or seven years old.

The United States has always been a haven for persons being persecuted because of their religious or political beliefs. The Pilgrims, who settled at Plymouth in 1620, were the first refugees to reach these shores. Since that time, millions more have come to this country to escape tyranny and to be free to live according to their beliefs.

But today's world is one of increasing political, economic, and religious turmoil. Since 1975, refugees or persons claiming to be refugees have arrived in the United States in far greater numbers than during any similar span of years in the nation's history. Because of a nationally felt obligation stemming from the war in Vietnam, over 750,000 Indochinese refugees have come to the United States

A Guatemalan child newly arrived at a refugee camp in Mexico.

in official government resettlement programs. In 1980, the United States accepted over 120,000 persons expelled or let go from Cuba by the government of Fidel Castro.

Deeply concerned about the heavy flow of refugees into the country, the United States Congress in 1980 passed a law which defined a refugee as a person ". . . who is unable or unwilling . . . to return to his country because of persecution or a well-founded fear of persecution on account of race, religion, nationality, membership in a particular social group, or political opinion." Under this

Vietnamese refugees rescued after being adrift in the South China Sea.

law, people persecuted for any of those reasons anywhere in the world can ask for refugee status in the United States, but the law limits the number of refugees who can enter the country in any one year to fifty thousand. The president, however, can admit an unlimited additional number of refugees if he believes it is necessary to do so. The fifty thousand limit has been exceeded in most years since the bill was passed.

Refugees are the most vulnerable immigrants to this country or any country because they have had to flee from their homeland with little more than the clothes they wore. They are cut off from family and friends with no way to communicate with them. They have lost their culture, of which language is such a vital part. In most cases they have spent long, hard months in refugee camps. Most vulnerable of all are refugee children who have left their country without their parents or who have lost them in the hazardous escape.

The U.S. government and all private welfare agencies that work with refugees have shown a serious concern for the Southeast Asian children living in refugee camps without parents. In 1984 the State Department and the Immigration and Naturalization Service sent a joint message to all U.S. embassies in Southeast Asia reminding them that ". . . Unaccompanied Indochinese Minors in the refugee camps in Southeast Asia are a subject of profound humanitarian concern . . . the U.S. objective is to accept for resettlement its fair share of those unaccompanied minors who the United Nations High Commissioner for Refugees determines should be resettled. . . ."

Who are these young refugees? Why did they leave the countries where they were born? What happens to them in the refugee camps? What is happening to them in the United States? What is their future likely to be? Will the numbers of unaccompanied refugee children coming to America grow, lessen, or cease altogether?

To try to answer these questions, we talked with foster parents, with child welfare caseworkers, and with officials in programs set up to help the young refugees. But mainly we talked with the unaccompanied refugee minors themselves. Perhaps we did not find all the answers; but we found many, and we learned a great deal about courage and love.

2 "My Father Told Me Good-bye"

W E BEGAN with the most basic question of all: why would parents, like Tran's, send their children on a perilous journey from which there could be no return?

Chi Cong Thi Truon provided us with a broad brush answer. Cong is a Vietnamese bilingual caseworker at the Catholic Refugee Center in Tucson, Arizona. Cong's mother worked for an American missionary in Vietnam; the U.S. military evacuated her and her family to the United States just ten days before the fall of Saigon to the Communist army in 1975.

"Life is poor in Vietnam now for the families of men and women who worked with the Americans," Cong said, "and often for families whose fathers were in the South Vietnamese army or in the government. Many of the men were put in prison and in reeducation camps. Reeducation camps are really prisons, too, where the men are supposed to be taught to be Communists. When they are released, it is hard for them to get jobs. It is hard for their children to get a good education, especially to get into college. And their sons are put in the army. It is said that they are likely to be sent to dangerous places, like Cambodia where the Vietnamese army is fighting now."

"But why doesn't the whole family escape?" we asked. "Why are children sent out by themselves?"

"Sometimes the whole family escapes," Cong said, "but most escape from Vietnam is by boat, and to buy passage on a boat is very expensive, sometimes as high as two thousand dollars for each person. And the passage must be paid in gold. It is hard for a family to send even one person, and when only one can go, usually the oldest son is sent."

"At those prices, it's a wonder anyone can buy passage."

"When the Americans were in Vietnam, many people had jobs and made money," Cong said. "They did not put their money in banks. They bought gold, twenty-four karat gold, and they hid it. Now they use the gold to send out a son or more than one if there is enough gold."

And when there is no gold, what happens? We found the answer when we talked to two Vietnamese brothers who had been in the United States for three years. "We had a good home in Vietnam," said the older brother. "We had good furniture. My father is a furniture maker," he added proudly. "We had nice dishes and even a television set. But my father sold everything to get gold for us to go in the boat. There was nothing left. My uncle sold his house so that his sons could leave."

In story after story that we heard, the drive of parents to get their children out of Vietnam seemed so intense, so desperate that we wondered if there was not more behind their concern than education and even army service.

"There is more," a program official in Washington, D.C., told us. "Some of the parents are devout Buddhists. Some are devout Christians. They see their kids getting brainwashed by the Communists. Kids in the schools are actually taught to spy on their parents and report them if they say anything or do anything that's against the party line. It's Orwell's *1984*. Some mothers and fathers

A Vietnamese child is taken from a refugee boat onto a rescue ship.

are going to get their children out of that if they have to sell everything they own."

But Khai Van Le, a Vietnamese social worker for Catholic Family Services of Richmond, Virginia, gave us the clearest insight into the reason Vietnamese parents send their children out of that country at almost any cost.

"Life in Vietnam has changed so drastically under communism," Mr. Le said. "The Communists want to disrupt the family system that we have had for centuries. They say families are not important anymore. Youth belong to the party, not to parents. The party is responsible for their upbringing. Parents are responsible only for bearing children. Communists are trying to create a force of young people with allegiance only to the party. They begin to teach children from kindergarten that they must report anything that can be harmful to the party, even their own family.

"Parents lose their children if they stay in Vietnam. They lose their children if they go to America. Vietnamese people have mixed feelings about America because of the experience of the war. But to many Vietnamese, America stands for freedom and a chance to build a new life. They know there is a large Vietnamese community in the United States, so it's not like sending the child into a desert. There is a support system here. The children will become U.S. citizens and maybe the whole family can follow someday. Even if the family can't come to America, Vietnamese parents want what is best for their children, so they send them."

At least 50 percent of the young refugees we talked to had not had the slightest forewarning that they were going to be separated from their family, probably forever. One night they were simply put aboard an escape boat that would take them to a refugee camp— unless it capsized, was captured by the Vietnamese coast guard, or attacked by pirates. It seemed to us an act of extreme cruelty, and we said so to a former refugee camp worker who had seen many children arrive in the camps.

"Of course it's cruel," she agreed. "But it's an act of extreme love, too—to give up your children so they can have a chance at a better life. They would like to tell their children what's happening, but they're afraid to. If the child tells someone, his best friend maybe, the police may find out and grab the whole escape boat. Their gold is gone and the boy may be sent to a reeducation camp."

In some cases parents do tell their children what is going to happen. We talked with a boy named Lam who was only eleven when he was sent out. His older brother had tried to escape, but he had been caught and put in prison. "So my father told me I should go," Lam said and added matter-of-factly, "I tried three times before I got on a boat, but I never got caught."

We also met some young refugees who had made their own decision to escape and had then asked their parents for their approval and support. One of those was Tung, who was fourteen when he left Vietnam. He spent eight months in two different refugee camps; although he has been in the United States only a little over a year, he understands and speaks English well.

"My father was a captain in the South Vietnamese army," Tung told us. "He was put in prison for eight years after the war. My mother had a little store, and she sold medicine and other things to make a living for us. I have two younger brothers and a sister. When my father returned from prison, and I saw what had happened to him, I said that I wanted to leave Vietnam. My mother and father said that I should go.

"I knew that escape is very dangerous because the boats sometimes sink. For many months I trained for ocean endurance. I swam a long time every day and practiced to stay afloat. When I was ready I tried to escape, but I was caught and put in jail. I stayed there for twenty-one days before my mother paid money and bought my release.

"Then I tried again and got on a boat, and the price was two bars of gold. The boat was very small. Only eight people were in it. Two navy patrol boats saw us, but we pretended to be fishermen,

Tung today, outside his foster home in Tucson.

and they did not stop us. We were four days and nights on the sea. Our boat almost sank in a storm and then the engine stopped working. We were just drifting, but some Malaysian fishermen saw us and helped us get to the refugee camp on Pulau Bidong. I was ready to swim in the ocean, but I am glad I did not have to."

Of all the tragedies of war in Southeast Asia, the calamities of the Cambodian people are the most terrible. When the Communist faction, called Khmer Rouge and led by a man named Pol Pot, gained control of the country in 1975, they began a campaign of death and destruction against their own people that can only be called the work of madmen.

Estimations are that over half the adult male population of Cambodia was killed by the Khmer Rouge. Total deaths by massacre, starvation, and forced labor may have exceeded 2 million. Whole towns were destroyed. Children were taken from their parents and worked to death. In one village a mass grave holds the bodies of two thousand children. Piles of skulls could be seen throughout the country: 18,000 in one stack, 38,000 in another.

To escape this horror, tens of thousands of Cambodians fled from their country to take refuge in neighboring Thailand. Sometimes children, lone survivors in families that had been massacred, attached themselves to friends or even strangers in the flight to Thailand. In time many of them were taken from the refugee camps and brought to America as unaccompanied minors.

One girl was just thirteen when she was taken from her family and put in one of Pol Pot's infamous children's camps. She escaped from the camp, was shot in the back at the dangerous border crossing, and stayed for a year in a Thai refugee camp. Now she is living with a foster family in Boston. She does not know whether her mother, father, sisters, and brothers are alive or dead.

Pol Pot and the Khmer Rouge were defeated by invading Vietnamese armies in 1979, but confusion, fighting, and terror have continued in Cambodia. Leng and Alan (he has taken an American

Leng (left) and Alan opening presents at a Cambodian New Year celebration, while a caseworker's daughter looks on.

name) are brothers who fled into Thailand. Leng, the older, went first, and Alan followed a year later. His father guided him to the border.

"My father told me good-bye," Alan said, "and he told me to find my brother."

Today Leng and Alan are living together in Silver Spring, Maryland, in a group home for unaccompanied refugee minors run by Associated Catholic Charities.

The hope of a better life, a determination to escape political oppression: these are the powerful motives that have always brought refugees to America. These motives have not changed for parents in Southeast Asia who must make the cruel decision to give up their children in the hope that they will find their way to freedom.

3 The Refugee Camp

A LREADY the morning sun was hot. Mai lay on her cot on the girls' side of the bamboo-and-thatch hut where the unaccompanied children lived. She had been awake for over an hour, waiting for the wake-up call and thinking about the day to come, the day she would have her interview.

On the other side of the woven grass partition, the boys' side, Mai heard the young Catholic priest who lived with them softly recite his morning prayers. Soon he would wake everyone up for breakfast. She wished she had more time. I'm not ready, she thought. What if I make a mistake? What if I give the wrong answers and they don't let me go to America? What if I have to stay in this camp forever?

Mai was fourteen. She had been in the refugee camp two months, but the two months seemed to her like two years. She thought every day about her father and mother who lived near the city of Nha Trang in Vietnam. She thought about her older brother who was married and had a new baby, and she thought about her two younger sisters. Mai would remember forever the night her

21

father had put her on the small boat that took her away. She had been so sad and frightened that she could not speak, but she had not cried. She would never forget, either, the look of sadness on her father's face. But her father had decided this was the time for her to go because their good friends, Mr. and Mrs. Hai, would be on the refugee boat. She would not be entirely alone.

Seven other girls slept in the room with Mai. There were many more boys in the house, almost forty, she thought. All of them had come to the camp without parents or any adult relative to take care of them. They had been put in this special place with adults to supervise them. Mai talked to all of the girls and boys, but mostly she talked to Thanh.

Thanh was sixteen and had been in the camp for nine months. A Boy Scout troop had been organized in the camp, and Thanh was one of a group of older Scouts that had been sent to the dock to meet Mai's boat the day it arrived. Mai and fifteen other people had drifted in the South China Sea for two weeks before a French ship found them and brought them to the Vietnamese refugee camp on the island of Palawan in the Philippines. Mai was thirsty, hungry, and almost sick when they reached shore, but she would never forget the wonderful sight of the Vietnamese boys with their bright green neckerchiefs, welcoming them to the camp. Thanh had carried her plastic bag, the only possession she had, to the camp for her.

In the days and weeks that followed, many refugees in the camp had talked to Mai about the interviews that would decide the country to which she would be sent. They had given her all kinds of advice about what to say, but Thanh was the one she had listened to.

"Tell the truth," he said. "If you don't know the answer to a question, say you don't know. Don't try to make up an answer or say what you think they want to hear."

She would follow Thanh's advice, but now she thought, what if I say what they don't want to hear? What will happen to me then?

Young scouts recite the Scout Oath at a refugee camp on the island of Palawan.

The priest clapped his hands and called, "Everybody up!"

There was no more delaying. Mai got up and dressed quietly amidst the chatter of the other girls. She combed her long black hair and braided it carefully, making sure no stray hairs escaped. I wish I had my blue tunic and pants, she thought, as she looked down at the clean but faded T-shirt and pants she was wearing.

Mai forced down a few bites of breakfast and then left for her interview. Before reaching the main road of the camp, she passed the house of Mr. Nguyen and his family. The Nguyens had been in the camp for over two years, and no one knew if they would ever be accepted to go to another country. Mr. Nguyen had opened a noodle shop where he made wonderful soups full of vegetables and noodles and sometimes bits of shrimp. The Nguyens had four

Children in school at the refugee camp on the island of Palawan.

children, one of whom was Chung, a boy Mai's age. She did not like him because he laughed at the children in camp without parents. He said their families were so poor they could not escape together. But Mai could not see that the Nguyens' money was helping them get out of the refugee camp.

On the main road Mai passed children on their way to the different schools in the refugee camp. The younger children were going to a school run by Dutch nuns. For the older ones there was a school where they studied English and math and at the same time learned what an American high school was like. In a few days Mai would start in that school.

Now the camp was coming to life. Women gathered at the water pumps to fetch water for their houses or to wash clothes. Toddlers played together in the dirt around their mothers' feet. Men were coming from morning worship at the Buddhist temple, others from weekday mass at the Catholic church. They gathered at small coffeehouses to gossip about what was happening in Vietnam and about refugee policies in America. For most men there was no work in the camp, nothing to do all day but sit, think, and talk.

Mai turned a corner and approached the office of the United Nations High Commissioner for Refugees. She climbed the wooden stairs. A woman, whose name she knew was Miss Morrison, was sitting at a desk in the bright open room. On her desk were flowers, and on the walls were pictures in many colors. In a chair near the desk sat a Vietnamese woman.

"Mai," said the woman in Vietnamese, "sit down and answer the questions that Miss Morrison asks you. I will tell you what she says and then you will answer. I will translate what you say into English. Do not be afraid."

"I know you are afraid," Miss Morrison said, "but all I want to do is ask you some questions about your parents and your life in Vietnam. I know that many people have told you that some answers are better than others, but the best answer for you is the truth. Will you tell me what is true, Mai?"

"Yes, I will tell you," Mai said, and she was glad that Thanh had told her to tell the truth.

"I have seen your birth certificate that you brought," Miss Morrison said. "Do you have any other papers or documents?"

"No," Mai said.

"Do you have any relatives in the United States?"

"No, I do not know of any."

"Do you have any relatives in any country besides Vietnam? An uncle? An aunt?"

"My father did not tell me of any," Mai said.

Miss Morrison wrote briefly on the interview form. The first part of her job was to try to reunite a refugee with a family member in another country. "Family reunification" it was called. In Mai's case, as in so many, that would not be possible. Now would come the determination of whether Mai would qualify as a refugee under United States law.

"Mai, tell me what work your father does."

"My father works sometimes in the rice fields," Mai said, "and sometimes he helps to build houses."

"What did he do during the war?"

"My father—" Mai began and then stopped. She could not bring herself to go on. All her life she had been told never to speak of her father's position in the army of South Vietnam during the war.

"It is all right," the Vietnamese woman said to Mai. "You can tell Miss Morrison."

"My father was in the army," Mai said, "the South Vietnamese army. He was an officer in engineering."

"What happened to him after the war?" Miss Morrison asked.

"When the Communists came from the North, my father was put in prison," Mai said.

"For how long?"

"He was there for three years," Mai said and added, "I know because I was four years old when they took him away and seven when he came back."

Miss Morrison looked again at Mai's birth certificate. She was fourteen years old now. If her father had been put in prison or a reeducation camp in 1975, after the fall of Saigon, then Mai's memory about the time of her father's imprisonment was correct.

"You said your father was in the engineering corps in the army. Was he an engineer?"

"He was an engineer," Mai said. "He went to Dalat University."

"But after prison he did not work as an engineer?"

"No. They would not let him. He could only work in the rice fields and sometimes building houses, but just as a worker."

"Now, Mai," said Miss Morrison, "tell me why your father sent you away from Vietnam."

"He wants me to have an education like he had," Mai said

without hesitating. "He hopes I will be a doctor and I hope so, too. But he knows that the Communists will not let me go to the university because I am the daughter of a South Vietnamese army officer."

"Do you have an older brother, Mai?"

"Yes," Mai said. "I have one older brother."

"Why was he not sent from Vietnam instead of you?"

"He is married and has a new baby," Mai said.

Miss Morrison wrote again on the interview form. Mai's case might turn out to be easier than many. In order to qualify as a refugee under the United States Immigration Act of 1980, a person must prove that he or she has been persecuted because of political beliefs, religion, race, or social group—or has good reason to fear such persecution. A child who is denied education because of her father's past army service would qualify.

"Mai," Miss Morrison said, "you will be interviewed by other people during the next few weeks. These people will make a file about you which they will give to the United States Immigration and Naturalization Service—the INS. Then the INS people will talk to you. Tell them the truth, like you did with me." Miss Morrison smiled. "Don't worry. I think everything will be all right."

When Mai left the United Nations office, she was weak with relief, but she felt much better than she had when she went in. Now she hurried back to the house for unaccompanied refugee children to tell Thanh what had happened.

The refugee camps of Southeast Asia today bear almost no resemblance to those that were thrown together literally overnight in 1975. Fear of death, imprisonment, and life under communism caused a mass exodus from Vietnam and, shortly after that, from Cambodia and Laos. Once the "boat people" and the "land people" reached Thailand, Malaysia, Indonesia, and the Philippines, they were put into hastily organized refugee camps. These camps were overcrowded and without sanitary facilities. The refugees lived in makeshift tents

Teen-age boys play basketball at the camp on Palawan.

or hovels made of mud, tree branches, packing cases, and anything else that could serve as a roof or a wall. There was never enough food, and clothing and medicine were almost completely lacking. Death and despair were a constant part of camp life.

Thailand, Malaysia, Indonesia, and the Philippines are poor countries of "first asylum" that could not accept the hundreds of thousands of refugees permanently. The United States responded to the emergency and between April and December of 1975 alone airlifted 130,000 refugees from the camps to permanent resettlement in America. Other countries helped but took much smaller numbers of refugees.

Since 1975 the flow of refugees into the camps has continued as has their resettlement in the United States and other countries. With the passing years, however, the camps have become much

Children bathing in a Vietnamese refugee camp in the Philippines.

more organized and the living much improved under the management of the United Nations High Commissioner for Refugees and with the help of many international relief organizations such as the Red Cross and CARE.

Small houses and barracks have replaced shanties. Food is plain but adequate in amount. Every camp has reasonably well-staffed and stocked medical clinics. Schools have been started, temples and churches established. Youth groups and athletic activities help keep children and teen-agers occupied in some camps. Some refugees even run small businesses such as coffeehouses and supply stores.

Camp life is still hard and often monotonous, but many people believe that the camps now are not a bad place for a young unaccompanied refugee to be for a few months before being resettled permanently in the United States or some other country. Usually he or she will have a chance to learn some English, find out more about America, and make at least a little adjustment to being separated from family and friends.

But sometimes the months of waiting in camp stretch on far too long. As the refugee emergency of the first two or three years ended and the camps improved, the U.S. government and other countries became more careful as to whom they gave refugee status. From the time a person enters a refugee camp, an information file is compiled about him. Any documents he brings—such as birth certificate or army records—will be put in it. Sometimes a person is even asked to send for some record or piece of information in Vietnam, even though it may be months in coming or may never come.

When the file is as complete as it can be made, U.S. Immigration and Naturalization Service agents will interview the person seeking asylum in America and review his file. If a person is accepted by the INS, he or she will be processed for entry into the United States. If the person is rejected, however, there is no appeal unless new solidly documented information comes to light. If a refugee is rejected by the INS, caseworkers begin to search for another country that will take him.

Sometimes a refugee cannot find any country to accept him. There are many reasons for this: he may have a known or suspected criminal record; he may be considered a poor health risk; he may have been a troublemaker in camp. More likely, the interviewers may decide that the person is not really a refugee in the sense that he was being persecuted or had a reasonable fear of being persecuted. They may decide that he wanted to leave his country simply to improve his economic condition.

Some people, like the Nguyens, spend years in the camps. They have exhausted all possibilities for resettlement. The country where their camp is located won't take them, and they can't return to their home country. They start businesses in camp, go to school, get married, have children—and they wait.

On a day just three months from the day of her first interview, Mai walks to the airstrip that has been built beside the refugee camp on the island of Palawan. An airplane of Philippine Airlines waits there to take her and a dozen other unaccompanied refugee children to Manila. At Manila airport, they will be transferred to an American plane that will take them to the United States. Mai knows that she is going to live with a family in a place called Boston. She is excited and afraid, and she wishes she knew something about Boston.

Mai is also sad. She will miss friends she has made in the refugee camp. Thanh walks to the airstrip with her. He has just been told by Miss Morrison that he has been approved to go to America, but he will not leave until next month. A long search for an uncle who went to America years ago finally has been successful, and Thanh will live with him. Thanh will live in New York.

"I have looked on a map," Thanh says. "New York is not far from Boston."

"I will write you when I reach Boston," Mai tells him, and then she walks with the others to the big blue and red airplane.

4 Before They Arrive

FEW unaccompanied refugee minors know anything about the hard work and money that are required to prepare for their coming to America, to support them through their years of dependency, and to watch over their progress. A number of organizations are concerned with their well-being, among them the American Council for Nationality Services, Church World Services, the Hebrew Immigrant Aid Society, and the International Rescue Committee. Except in California, almost all placements of young refugees into foster care are handled by two national voluntary resettlement agencies: the Lutheran Immigration and Refugee Service (LIRS) and the United States Catholic Conference (USCC). Placements in California are arranged by the state Child Welfare Department.

The USCC and LIRS resettlement programs are carried out through their local charitable and social services offices in many cities throughout the United States. The local staff is usually small: a director, two or three caseworkers, and a secretary. Most directors and caseworkers have professional social welfare backgrounds, and one or more of the caseworkers usually are Vietnamese.

A young Vietnamese girl at a welcome party at the Connections office in Virginia.

Before a child arrives from one of the refugee camps, the local office will receive from USCC or LIRS headquarters in New York whatever information is available about him or her: name, age, sex, nationality, state of health, perhaps details about education and family in the home country. With this, often sparse, information in hand, the local staff's task is to find the best possible home for the young refugee who will soon arrive at the airport.

Because most unaccompanied refugee children and teen-agers have parents still alive in their home country, they cannot be adopted by Americans. Even when it is believed that the child's parents are dead, proof of death is difficult or even impossible to get. This means that the young refugee must live with *foster parents*. Foster parents are persons who agree to let a child live in their home and to provide parental care, even though the child is not related to them by blood or legal ties.

Legal responsibility for the unaccompanied refugee minors remains with the Lutheran and Catholic organizations, and they must report regularly to the state supervising agency and to the courts about the welfare of the children. Caseworkers visit at least once a month with the foster parents and refugee children and help with problems that may develop. Most placements are successful; but if the foster parents decide they made a mistake in volunteering to provide foster care, they can ask LIRS or USCC to take the child back. And if the LIRS or USCC staffs decide that the relationship is not working out, they can find new foster parents for the child.

Clearly then, one of the most important jobs of the refugee staff is to find foster homes that will provide good care for the unaccompanied refugee children until they reach the legal age of adulthood. In most states that is eighteen; in a few it is twenty-one. But when the bonding of foster parents and foster children is really successful, the relationship will not end at some official cutoff date.

The search for foster parents goes on all the time. Notices are placed in local church publications and on church bulletin boards. The refugee office tries to get newspapers and radio stations to carry stories about the need for people to help in the program. But probably most new foster parents volunteer because they have friends or acquaintances who are already foster parents. They have a concrete example to study, and they decide they would like to be a part of the program.

The refugee office staff carries out a thorough study of a potential foster home before any assignment of a refugee child is made to it. The home is visited at least three times. Prospective foster parents are interviewed carefully; children and any other family members are talked to. The house itself is inspected to make

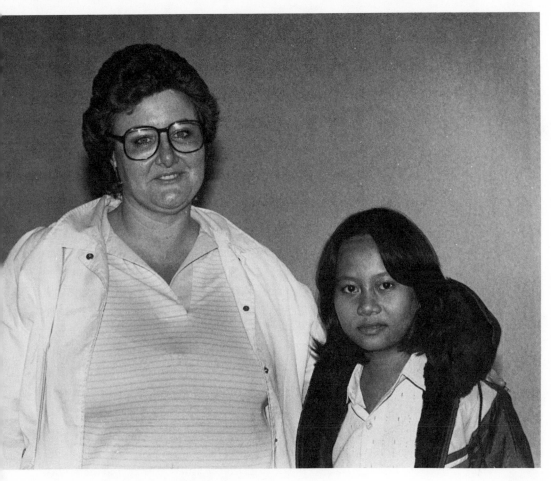

A newly arrived refugee with her new foster mother.

sure there is room for an additional person or persons. The history of the family's stability and even financial condition is reviewed. The best time to prevent a mistake in placement is before the refugee child arrives.

Once prospective foster parents are chosen, they must go through a preparatory program, usually twelve hours or more, before they receive a refugee child. The course includes background information about who unaccompanied refugee minors are and about why they have arrived at refugee camps without their parents. The course provides information on what the child's probable expectations are, and foster parents-to-be are encouraged to think about what their expectations are. Persons who are already foster parents of refugee children are brought into the training to share their experiences and to talk about what they have learned in bridging the vast cultural gap between them and their foster child.

Money to take care of the children in foster homes is provided by the U.S. government through various congressional acts, most recently the Refugee Act of 1980. Funds are channeled through state child welfare agencies to the LIRS and USCC offices and then on to the foster parents.

Allowances for refugee foster children are different in each state because they are based on what the state pays for American children that courts place in foster care. In Arizona, for example, foster parents are initially given $496 per month for each refugee foster child. After four months that figure is reduced to $315 per month. By the end of the first year it will go down to $268 per month and stay at that rate. A monthly clothing allowance of $27.50 is given, as well as a spending money allowance of $14 a month. Refugee children are given a special clothing allowance of $300 when they arrive since they have almost no clothes when they get off the plane. Special medical expenses are also provided for.

While these allowances are adequate, most foster parents soon find that they are reaching into their own pockets to supplement the money given by the government. "You want them to have what your own kids have," says one foster father. "Bikes, soccer balls, books, presents, guitars—and guitar lessons. And, of course, they go on vacations with you. And after they learn how the phone works, they can spend a bundle calling friends in other cities that they knew in the refugee camp!"

"And clothes," adds a foster mother. "Once they really start eating good food, they grow so fast you can't believe it. They can run through three months of clothing allowance in a month."

Refugee foster parents are asked by program staff to think long and hard about why they want to bring a child from a totally

One of the Speers' foster sons.

different culture into their home. Our conversations with many foster parents made clear that they have thought about why they took this demanding step, but answers are not easy to express.

"Our son was at college, and we had this empty room," says Bob Speers, a foster father in Tucson. "Every day we saw the empty bed there, and we knew about the refugee foster child program. There is so much wrong in the world that we can't do anything about, but taking in a Vietnamese child was something we could do."

Now Bob Speers and his wife, Charlotte, have two teen-age Vietnamese foster sons.

Jill and Jim Rich answered a newspaper advertisement for a temporary home for unaccompanied refugee minors, a place where they could stay for a short time until their permanent home was ready. Jill and Jim's motive seemed to be curiosity as much as anything, an opportunity for a different cultural experience. Now, after a year, they are permanent foster parents of two Vietnamese teen-agers and still take in temporary refugee children. "It *was* a new experience," says Jill, "and worthwhile. We're in this for good."

Walter and Betsy Nunn of Arlington, Virginia, have three foster children from the refugee camps of Southeast Asia. With their two adopted American children, they have a very full house.

"Why did we bring them into our family?" says Walter, with a little shake of his head. "It's something you feel, not something you talk about."

Most of the foster parents we talked to would agree with Walter Nunn. The decision to take in a refugee child was made as much with their hearts as with their heads.

5   Into a Strange Land

I WANTED to go back to the refugee camp," Thua said. "I wanted to go back the same day I got to my new home in America. The next day I wanted to go back more. Does that sound crazy? For one whole year I wanted to leave the refugee camp more than anything. Every day I wanted to leave that camp. Then I am in America and I want to go back. Maybe I was crazy. But now I think I was just afraid. So afraid I could not think or hardly move. More afraid than when I was on a boat in the ocean. More afraid than when I came to the refugee camp."

We were sitting in the living room of Thua's foster home in the suburbs of Washington, D.C. He had been there now for two years. He spoke English rapidly, still heavily accented but easy to understand. We knew something of Thua's background. Three years ago, when Thua was just thirteen, his father had decided that they should escape from Vietnam, just the two of them. His father had worked for the American Embassy in Saigon and after the war had been put in a reeducation camp for three years. He was still watched by the government, and he felt that he and his son would always live

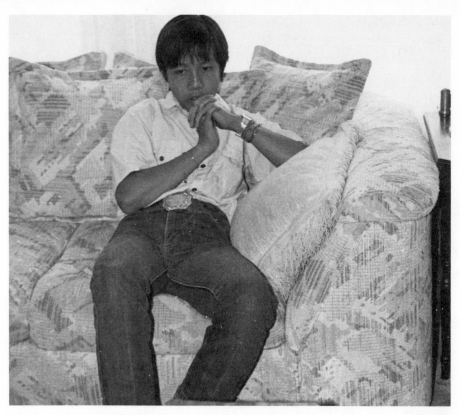

Thoughts of home in Vietnam?

under a shadow in Vietnam. Thua's mother was dead, and his two brothers were grown and had families of their own.

On the night of their escape, two small boats were to take the escapees to a larger boat waiting offshore. When Thua and his father reached the boats, there was room for only one more person in the boat about to leave. Thua was put into it. He reached the large boat, but the second small boat carrying his father was intercepted by the coast guard and turned back to shore. The big escape boat immediately left for the high seas, and Thua ended up in a Malaysian refugee camp by himself.

Thua was terribly depressed, worrying about what had happened to his father. After six months in the refugee camp, Thua learned that his father had been put in jail but had been let out after three months and that he seemed to be well. Thua felt a little better, but then he received another disappointment. He had an aunt living in Paris and had hoped that he would be sent to live with her. But the camp authorities were finally notified that the aunt was unable to take responsibility for him. When, after a year, Thua was finally cleared for resettlement in the United States, he was suffering not only from the separation from his father but also from the disappointment of not being able to join his aunt.

"Too much," was all Thua said when we talked to him about his dangerous escape from Vietnam and his year of anxiety and uncertainty in the refugee camp.

Then this boy just turned fourteen, who had never seen an airplane before except in the sky, was put on a giant 747 and flown into a world he could not even begin to imagine. It might have helped if there had been other refugee children on the flight to the United States, but that day there were not.

"What do you remember most about the flight?" we asked him.

"Wait," Thua said. He went to his room and came back with a small white card. "This is what I remember most."

The card, about three by five inches, was an identification tag. At the top were the words UNACCOMPANIED MINOR. Under that was Thua's full name and a 24-hour phone number to call in case of problems or questions.

"It was pinned to my shirt front," Thua said. "No one else on the airplane had one. That is what I remember most. Maybe someone told me what it was, but if they did, I did not understand. I did not know what it was, and it made me more afraid."

Thua went back to his room and returned carrying a heavy jacket with a red, white, and blue patch on the right shoulder. The jacket looked quite new. "In San Francisco, the people who met me and helped me change planes gave me this jacket," he said. "I wore it on the plane that day, but I have never worn it since. All refugee minors get a jacket like this in San Francisco. But nobody wears it after that."

"Why not?" we asked.

Thua shrugged. "That patch," he said. "It just shows you're a refugee kid."

"You said you were more afraid when you came to America than when you escaped from Vietnam or when you first went into the refugee camp. How can that be?"

"I don't know," Thua said. "Maybe I was most afraid in the boat. But I was with Vietnamese people. I could talk to them. In the refugee camp, we were all the same. I could talk to people and understand them. There was not so much food, but it was food like I had always had. The weather was like the weather in Vietnam. The refugee camp was not good, but I knew where I was.

"Snow was coming down the day the plane brought me here. I knew about snow, but I had never seen snow. I had never been in cold like the cold here. My foster mother and father brought me to this house. I had never seen a house like it. Rugs on all the floors. I had my own room with my own television set and my own bathroom. When I turned on the water in the bathroom, I burned my hand.

"My foster parents were kind. They talked to me and showed me everything, but I could not understand one word. I had learned some words of English in the refugee camp, but I could not remember one word. I wanted to say something nice, but I had no words. That night for our first meal they tried to have food I would like, but everything looked strange to me, even the rice. I ate some rice, but I did not like it.

"When I went to bed, I did not think I could ever get up. I stayed in bed for three days. I just got up to go to the bathroom and to drink water. When I was not asleep, I pretended to be asleep so I would not have to see anybody or do anything. Sometimes my foster mother or father came in to talk to me, but I would not look at them. I was afraid if I got up I would do something stupid, and they would send me back to the refugee camp."

"But you said you wanted to go back to the refugee camp."

The Breaszale family with foster sons.

"I said that, but it was not true. I was just afraid they would not like me and would send me back. But finally I got out of bed."

Almost without exception the unaccompanied refugee children who come to America bring with them the same fears that Thua had. Bill and Sue Breaszale are foster parents in Tucson, Arizona, with three Vietnamese foster sons. Bill and Sue have come to know many other unaccompanied refugee children and teen-agers in Tucson over the months that they have had their foster sons.

"These kids are all emotionally bankrupt when they get here," Bill says. "I have never seen such fright as when they first arrive."

Loretta Tracy agrees. An experienced social worker, Loretta is in charge of the unaccompanied refugee minors program for Associated Catholic Charities in Tucson. She has met dozens of bewildered young refugees at the airport. "They have come to the end of their

Loretta Tracy is in charge of the Tucson unaccompanied refugee minors program. The Tracy family includes two teen-age refugees.

emotional rope," she says. "Our job is to find a good home for them and then to stay in close touch with them and their foster parents as they get their new lives started."

In a number of cases, newly arrived unaccompanied refugee children go first to a temporary home. This may be because a permanent home has not yet been found for them or is not ready to receive them. A large temporary home in Peoria, Illinois, is called Tha Huong, which means "Home Away from Home." At any one time from seven to forty young refugees may be living there. Most of them stay at Tha Huong for three to seven months before being placed in permanent foster care. While they are at Tha Huong they study English, receive careful health checkups, and learn about

Rose DuTremaine and her Vietnamese foster sons in their Tucson home.

American customs. Since 1979, over five hundred refugee children have passed through Tha Huong. Another large temporary home is located in New Orleans.

In most places, however, a temporary placement, when needed, is made in a home that already has one or two refugee foster children. Such a placement may last from a few days to three months, but the average is about two weeks. Going into a temporary home and then being shifted to a permanent foster home might seem to be just one extra, confusing move for a refugee child, but there can be advantages.

Jill Rich, speaking of young refugees who come temporarily into her home, says: "Complete acceptance is what we try to give them. These kids are so confused, so tired when they arrive. They need some time to rest and gain a little confidence. Sometimes new foster parents, with the best intentions, try to push them too fast.

"If they want to sleep or just stay in bed for a couple of days, we let them. If they don't want to eat, we don't try to force them. When they cry, we're there if they want us, but we don't try to stop them. They have plenty to cry about. Little by little we bring them into our family."

The Riches' two Vietnamese foster children play an important role in helping new arrivals gain a first sense of confidence and security. Trung and Hieu are brother and sister. Trung is sixteen; Hieu (her name is pronounced *Hue*) is fifteen. They have lived with Jill and Jim Rich for almost a year, and their experiences as refugees can match those of any newcomer to the Rich home.

Trung and Hieu were sent out of Vietnam by their father, who despaired of their ever having a decent life in that country. They were afraid and did not want to leave their home, but they obeyed their father. One night he put them on a boat that carried almost a hundred other escapees, and he gave them a small bag and a picture of himself. On the fifth day at sea, with almost no water or food left aboard, their boat encountered Malaysian fishermen who showed them the way to a refugee camp.

Trung and Hieu lived in the Malaysian camp for ten months. They stayed in a longhouse, which was really a barracks, and their chief memories of the camp now are that they were hungry much of the time. They were given rice, noodles, vegetables, and sometimes chicken, but they remember nights when they went to sleep thinking about food. They slept on mats and wore clothes issued by the camp.

At last they were cleared to come to the United States and to live with foster parents in Tucson. They changed planes at the international airport in Los Angeles, and their new plane made a

Trung and Hieu.

stop in Phoenix before going on to Tucson. Thinking they were to get off at the first stop, Trung and Hieu left the plane. There was no one to meet them, of course, and they wandered helplessly in the Phoenix airport for hours before an airline attendant noticed them and knew that something was wrong. When they were finally put back aboard a plane to Tucson, they were as bewildered and frightened as they had been since they left Vietnam.

Trung can find humor in their arrival experience now. "In Phoenix they found a Chinese man to talk to us and find out who we were," he remembers. "But the man could not speak Vietnamese, and we could not speak Chinese. We just looked at each other."

Hieu makes the important point. "We can talk to the new ones who come here," she says, "and they can talk to us. We know how they feel. We really know."

Most important, the "new ones" can look at Hieu and Trung and perhaps begin to imagine themselves as a part of an American family.

6 Depression: An Emotional Time Bomb

T HE FIRST days of paralyzing fear pass. The newly arrived
refugee child begins to come to the table at mealtimes. He does
not eat much, but, when his foster mother asks him if he likes the
food, he says yes. The boy's name is Phuong. When the family
members ask him if they are saying it right, he says yes. Phuong
wears his new clothes, the same kind that his foster brother Tim
wears: jeans, cotton pullover shirt, wool plaid jacket, and sneakers.
His foster father asks him if he likes the clothes, and Phuong says
yes.

Tim tries to teach Phuong to throw and catch a football. He
finally does catch a few passes but has little success throwing the
odd-shaped ball. A bit of English Phuong learned in the refugee
camp is coming back. "Not like soccer ball," he says.

Within a week of his arrival at his new home, Phuong is enrolled
in school. A social worker from Lutheran Immigration and Refugee
Service goes with him the first day to help the guidance counselor
and teachers decide the best program for him. Phuong is fourteen
but says he went to school only three years in Vietnam. He is put

49

into high-intensity English language study and a special mathematics course. Tim goes to the same school, and for the first two days he helps Phuong through the maze of halls and the bewildering rush of students at the change of classes. Tim also makes sure that Phuong knows where to catch the bus after school.

Several other refugee teen-agers go to Phuong's school. Most escaped from Vietnam with their parents and brothers and sisters, but one boy, a Cambodian, came by himself like Phuong. Phuong soon meets him but, since they do not speak the same language, they can talk to each other only in the few words of English they have learned. Once after school Phuong goes home with a Vietnamese acquaintance. He meets the boy's mother and father and young brother and sister, and he stays for a Vietnamese dinner. When he returns to his own home later that evening, he is very quiet.

But Phuong seems to be doing well. He studies hard, both at school and at home in the evenings. He still talks very little, but, with some encouragement, he begins to say a few things at the dinner table. They talk about school and about the camp in Thailand where he stayed for six months. His foster parents know from the camp records furnished the Lutheran office that Phuong has a mother and a father and two sisters in Vietnam, but they cannot get Phuong to talk about them. Still, his foster mother and father agree, Phuong is moving smoothly into his new life. They have already grown attached to him and are pleased.

Then one day Phuong comes home from school, goes to his room, and closes the door. When he does not come to the table for dinner, his foster mother raps on his door. "Dinner is ready, Phuong," she says.

Phuong answers without opening the door. "Not hungry."

"Are you feeling all right?" his foster mother asks.

"Yes," he says. "Not hungry."

Phuong does not come out of his room at all that night, but the next morning he seems no different than usual. He eats breakfast and walks to the bus stop with Tim. That evening, however, he again goes directly to his room and does not come out for dinner. The same thing happens the next day and the next, and throughout the weekend he comes out of his room only to get food from the refrigerator and to use the bathroom. He does not eat with the family or say more than a few words to them.

Phuong's foster parents are worried, but, when they try to talk to him, he says that nothing is wrong. He tells them he is studying. On the following Monday, very late at night, Phuong's foster mother hears Vietnamese music coming from his room. She had put a radio and cassette player, together with a number of tapes, in his room before he arrived; but there had been no tape of Vietnamese music.

The next morning she asks Phuong about it. "Dong gave me a tape," he says. Dong is his Vietnamese friend, whose family he visited.

"I'm glad you have some Vietnamese music," his foster mother tells him, "but you mustn't play it so late at night."

"Okay, Mom," Phuong says.

His foster mother smiles. She always likes to hear "Mom," even though she knows it is the term all young unaccompanied refugees use.

But the Vietnamese music continues each night behind the door of Phuong's room. He keeps it low, but his foster mother still hears it. Now she is extremely worried, and she goes to the Vietnamese caseworker at the Lutheran office and tells her about the strange change in Phuong's behavior.

"We thought we were doing so well," she says, "and then all of a sudden he just put up a wall to keep us out. And the music he plays every night—that same tape over and over. I know something is wrong."

"I will talk to him," the caseworker says.

Since she talked to him several times soon after he arrived, the caseworker already knows a good deal about Phuong. She knows that his mother was very sick when he left Vietnam. He had told his parents he did not want to leave while his mother was sick, but

they both told him it was time to go. They had a friend with a boat
who would take him for little money, and there might be no other
chance. The day he arrived in America, the caseworker helped
Phuong write a letter to his parents, but his foster mother says that
no answer has come.

"Letters from Vietnam take long," the caseworker tells her.
And she adds, "If they come."

That night the caseworker goes to Phuong's room and talks to
him. She tells him that his foster mother is very worried because
he is not eating properly; she is afraid he will get sick. Phuong says
he is not sick. The caseworker says his foster mother is also worried
because he stays up late at night playing music when he should be
asleep. Phuong does not want to talk about the music; but they are
speaking the Vietnamese language, and he can say what he cannot
say in English.

"One night I was studying," he tells the caseworker, "and I
heard my mother crying."

"Perhaps you were asleep and heard your mother crying in a
dream," the caseworker says.

"No," Phuong says, "I was sitting at this desk, and I was not
asleep. I heard her crying. She is still sick, and she wants me to
come home."

"How do you know it was your mother?" the caseworker asks.

"I have heard her cry before," Phuong says. "In our home in
Vietnam. I know."

"Did she tell you she wants you to come home?" the caseworker
asks.

"She did not tell me," Phuong answers, "but I know."

The caseworker asks, "Have you heard your mother cry since
that first night?"

"No," Phuong says, "but I will be here when she comes again."

"And the music," the caseworker asks. "Why do you play it
every night?"

"So my mother will hear it," Phuong says.

Phoung is caught in an emotional crisis called depression. It is a crisis that probably nine out of every ten unaccompanied refugee children pass through during their adjustment to life in America. Sometimes the depression is so severe that the child must be placed in a psychiatrist's care; but in most cases the period of emotional upset can be worked through with the help of the foster family, caseworkers and staff psychologists, teachers, and friends.

Depression is a feeling of sadness or discouragement, often both of those feelings together. Everyone has such feelings from time to time, but in the case of true depression, they will seldom go away without special help. Depression is usually a problem for young refugees not when they first arrive but after they have been making an effort to adjust in their new homes for several weeks or even months.

Depression may show itself in a number of ways. The most common sign probably is that the young refugee, like Phuong, may begin to stay more and more in his or her room and talk to other members of the family as little as possible. Having trouble getting to sleep may be another sign or sleeping too much or having nightmares. Sometimes depression expresses itself as a wild, almost uncontrollable anger. Sometimes it shows up as appetite loss or being confused or being afraid to do things. Depression often reveals itself as a feeling of sadness so deep that the person cannot help crying.

Dr. Daniel D. Lee is a clinical psychologist who also happens to be Vietnamese. He was educated in the United States but was teaching in Vietnam until the collapse of the South Vietnamese government. Since then he has spent much of his time in the United States in counseling and mental health programs for Indochinese refugees, including unaccompanied minors. We talked with Dr. Lee about young refugees who enter the country alone.

"Look at it this way," Dr. Lee said. "They have lost their parents, their brothers and sisters, all at once. They were with them one day, and the next day they are gone. Maybe gone forever.

Dr. Daniel Lee with a group of teen-age unaccompanied refugees.

Maybe they will never see any of them again. That is a terrible loss, and the grief that it brings is terrible. And that is not the only loss the refugee child suffers. He suffers the loss of his whole culture, the loss of everything that is familiar to him, of everything that might make the loss of his family more bearable.

"So while he is grieving over this double loss of family and culture, he must learn to live in a new, strange country. Even when he arrives here, he is exhausted from the escape by sea or land and from having survived for months in a refugee camp. But there is no time to rest. From the first day he must begin to learn a new language, to live with people who know nothing about him or his customs, to eat new food, to find his way in a kind of school he never dreamed of, to wear heavy clothes in cold weather, to sleep in a room by himself when all his life he had slept with his whole family. And all the time he is thinking about his family and wishing he were with them."

Dr. Lee then talked about the differences between some American and Vietnamese values and approaches to life. "In America," he said, "truth means that you tell a person what you really think and feel. But to a Vietnamese the essence of truth is to maintain harmony. You avoid problems by agreeing. You say you like something when you don't if you think agreeing will avoid conflict. You say you understand something when you don't so that you won't be a bother.

"An American foster mother once said to me, 'These Vietnamese children will yes you to death.' And I said to her, 'You must learn the different meanings of yes to a Vietnamese.' And the Vietnamese smile—there may be a hundred different meanings to it. Foster parents must learn to read faces.

"An American father and mother want their children to look them in the eye. To a Vietnamese child that is impolite. Americans are taught to stand up for their rights. Vietnamese children are taught not to be assertive. These are just a few of the cultural differences that the Vietnamese refugee child must learn to deal with. There are so many more."

On the subject of raw human emotions that drive the unaccompanied refugee child into depression, Dr. Lee was most specific. "We have already talked about grief. That emotion overlays all others. But for some there is also guilt when they hear that their family in Vietnam is suffering or that their father is in jail. They may feel guilt if they get poor grades in school because they know they were sent here to get a good education.

"Anger. It is a powerful emotion for many. Anger because they were torn from their family. Anger because they do not understand why their father and mother made them leave Vietnam. Anger because they cannot understand English and cannot tell people how they feel. Fear, not only for themselves but for what may be happening to their families. Loneliness. Insecurity. Any of these emotions, or all of them, may push the refugee child, in the country by himself or herself, into depression."

When Dr. Lee counsels unaccompanied refugee children and teen-agers, he tries to help them sort out and understand these emotions and to talk about their feelings rather than repress them. "I try to help them accept what they cannot change," he said, "and I hope I help them make some sense out of what has happened to their lives."

Helping unaccompanied refugee minors fight depression is a task for everyone who is a part of their lives. It is a battle they must finally win for themselves, and almost all do; but the help of well-informed foster parents and foster brothers and sisters, of trained caseworkers, of teachers, and of phychologists like Dr. Lee, is essential.

And finally it is in other young refugees like themselves that they often can find a critical help. In most places where a number of unaccompanied refugee minors have found foster homes they come together from time to time to talk about what they are doing, what is happening to them, how they are dealing with problems that they have. During a meeting in one Pennsylvania community, the refugee children came up with these practical, down-to-earth suggestions that had helped them:

—Talk to other people who are willing to listen and also share their feelings with you; you will know that you are not alone.

—Go for a walk; look at nature; you will see things that you will think are beautiful, ugly, peaceful, scary, surprising.

—Listen to sad songs and let yourself cry; listen to other music and let yourself feel the rhythm inside.

—Play sports and games; when you need to let go of your

anger, hit a tennis ball or a volleyball, kick a soccer ball, throw or bat a baseball; enjoy the feeling of playing with a team.

—Write a diary; writing helps to put the thought that you have out of your head, and then you can close the book and put it away; you may want to share it with someone you trust or just keep it for yourself.

—Draw or paint pictures; make something with your hands, learn a craft, something to keep or give away; decorate your room with permission from your foster parents.

—Go places with your foster family and new friends; feel the fear and do it anyway; most times you will be glad that you did.

—Spend some time alone to think and to pray. Learn about a religion that interests you. Attend religious services with your family and/or friends.

Phuong made it through his depression. He made it with the help of his foster parents, teachers, and caseworker. Perhaps the turning point was the day Tim brought home a soccer ball and asked Phuong to teach him how to kick it and head it. Phuong had played soccer almost from the time he could walk, and Tim could not have had a better teacher. That first day they practiced until dark, and Phuong ate his dinner at the table that night.

Phuong still takes high-intensity English training, but he has been "mainstreamed" in some of his classes at school. When Phuong at last received a letter from his parents in Vietnam, he was overjoyed to learn that his mother was no longer ill. But he had already won his battle with depression without that wonderful news.

7 | Learning and Changing

T HE DAILY task of the unaccompanied refugee minor is to learn how to get along in his strange new world: how to understand what is being said to him and how to make himself understood; how to learn the mysterious rituals of school and become a good student; how to find his way around in a city that seems all noise, speed, and chaos; above all, how to deal with the bewildering mix of feelings he has every day about his new family, his new home, his new life.

Learning family routines and household responsibilities can be emotionally upsetting, especially for boys. In the countries they have come from, few have had to do household chores, which were always the work of mothers, grandmothers, and sisters. But in America the refugee boy quickly learns that he is expected to shoulder his share of the work necessary to keep the house running smoothly. He probably will be expected to keep his room clean, which means running the vacuum cleaner. He may be expected to take his turn setting the table, stacking dishes, taking out the trash, even walking the dog. He probably won't be asked to help in the kitchen with food, but some yard work is likely to be a part of his

5 8

responsibility. He won't be asked to do anything the rest of the family isn't doing, but he may not see it that way.

"I did not understand, and I was angry," a Vietnamese boy said. "Once I said to Mom, 'You just took me so you could have a servant.' My English was very poor then, and she did not know what I said. I am so glad because now I understand that doing work in the house is different here. I do not like it, but I understand."

Conforming to schedules for meals, homework, and bedtime can be a problem for some older teen-age refugee boys. Often they have grown accustomed to a good deal of independence in the refugee camps and even in their home countries where their father may have been in prison and their mothers away from home all day working. In their new home in America they may be restless and lonely because so little communication is possible. At school they usually find a few friends from their country and want to spend most of their time with them.

"I was like that," said a Laotian boy who has now been in the United States three years and will soon be going to college. "I never wanted to stay home. Many times I would not come home after school and I would not come home for dinner. Most nights I would go to a Laotian friend's house. Or I would meet one of them—I just had two friends—at Wendy's. We did not do anything, but we could speak our language and talk about Laos and what had happened to us.

"My schoolwork was bad. I was learning some English but not enough. Mom, my foster mother, had the caseworker talk to me many times, but I did not change. One night Mom said I could not go out because she knew there was a test the next day. I said I was going out anyway. She said if I did, she would ask my caseworker to move me to another foster home.

"I was very angry. 'I don't want to stay with you anymore,' I said. I went back to my room and slammed the door. I put on my coat and came back.

"Mom was sitting in a chair in the living room crying. I was very much ashamed. It just came over me when I saw her. I wanted to say I was sorry, but I did not know how. I stood there and then I said, 'I am not going out.' I went back to my room, and after that I changed. Not all at once, but I changed."

Establishing a good relationship with foster brothers and sisters may be harder than with foster parents. Usually the natural children have agreed to the refugee's coming into the family, but in almost all cases the idea and the final decision were those of the parents. Sometimes the natural children do resent having to share their parents' time and attention with the newcomer. More often, however, a feeling of awkwardness and intruding leads the newly arrived refugee to stay out of the way of other children in the family.

Time and the efforts of parents in planning activities for the whole family usually solve the problem, but the key always is how to get communication started. One fifteen-year-old Vietnamese boy named Duc told of the surprising way it happened in his case.

"I was worried when I learned there was a boy in my foster family. I did not know how he would feel about me being in his house. When I got there he said hello, but he was always busy doing things and going out with his friends, and I did not see him much.

"He would say, 'Hi, Duc,' in the morning when we ate breakfast in the kitchen, but sometimes we would not say anything to each other the rest of the day. I did not think he liked me. It is true I did not talk to him because in the beginning I was afraid to use the little bit of English I knew.

"One day when I came home from school, David—that is my foster brother—was in the living room. He said, 'Hi, Duc,' and then he said, '*Hom nay em hoc the nao?*'

"I could not believe what I had heard. He had said in Vietnamese, 'How was school today?' I said to David in English, 'What did you say?'

"And he said again, '*Hom nay em hoc the nao?*'

"I still could not believe it. 'You are speaking Vietnamese,' I said.

" 'You aren't speaking English, so I thought I would learn Vietnamese,' David said. 'I had a Vietnamese girl in my class teach me.'

"We both laughed, and it turned out that all the Vietnamese he had learned was that one sentence, but it was enough. After that I started to speak English to him, and it was easier than I thought. Now he helps me with English sometimes, and sometimes I can help him with math. He has his friends and I have mine, but David and I are friends."

While he is finding his way in a kind of homelife totally different from what he has ever known, the unaccompanied young refugee must at the same time learn to function in equally strange American schools. This double burden of learning new customs, new forms of behavior, new routines is a real overload, but there is no way that the learning at home and at school can be separated. He simply must work his way through both at the same time.

The first days of a refugee child or teen-ager in his new school are as frightening and confusing as the first days in his new home. They are a blur of shouting and laughing students rushing through the halls, of locker doors slamming, of bells ringing, of standing in cafeteria lines looking at food he does not want to eat, of trying to tell counselors and teachers how much and what kind of schooling he had in his country, of hoping he is on the right school bus home and that he will remember where to get off. Some schools have a buddy system, assigning someone who has already been through this trauma, to help the newcomer in the first days, and that is a great blessing.

Sooner than he believed possible the new refugee is into the school routine and on the long, hard road to becoming functional in English. He will study mathematics and perhaps other subjects in special tutoring, but most of his time will be spent in HILT, High-Intensity Language Training, or ESL, English as a Second Language. He will go at his own speed, for every refugee brings a different background to the class.

Regardless of background, each refugee student has memories of getting the strange new language under control. "I had studied English one hour a day for six months in refugee camp," recalled a Vietnamese boy named Duy, "and I had studied French in Vietnam for two years, because French is still taught in most of the schools there. After six months of HILT I was put into regular ninth grade classes. I could read and I understood okay, but I was afraid to say anything if I didn't have to.

"Then a time came when everyone in class had to get up and make a report. I told the teacher I couldn't do that, but she said she thought I could. The night before my talk I stayed up until three o'clock going over and over what I was going to say. When I went to bed, the words kept going through my mind, and I never got to sleep.

"When my turn came that day, I went up in front of the class and stood there and couldn't remember a thing. Not one word. My mind just wouldn't work in English. I wanted to sit down, but my legs wouldn't work, either. I just stood there. And then I started talking, but it wasn't English. It was Vietnamese. I made my whole five-minute talk in Vietnamese. I thought everyone would laugh, but no one did, and when I sat down, they clapped. Even the teacher.

"The next day I made my talk again, and that time English came out."

In time most refugee students will, like Duy, be mainstreamed into the regular school program. The pressure on many of them to excel in their studies will be great. Letters from home may urge them to make top grades so they can get into a good college. Often the young refugee pushes himself to the limit and beyond because he hopes

Dennis Hunt, psychologist and director of Connections, with a newly arrived Cambodian refugee.

that, by doing well, he at some future time will be able to bring other members of his family to the United States. Foster parents, too, sometimes contribute to the pressure by putting too much emphasis on grades.

"Some foster parents have false expectations when they take in Asian children," says Essa Reny, senior social worker for Connections, an organization responsible for unaccompanied refugee minors. "They have heard and read that Asians are such whizzes in school, so great in math and science. They say, 'Why aren't my kids getting straight *As*?' They forget that their foster children probably have come out of deprived backgrounds and may be suffering all kinds of psychological problems based on their past, their sudden separation from their parents, and their refugee camp experiences."

Still, successful school performance is important to the young refugee's future. A mixture of encouragement and understanding, carefully applied by counselors, teachers, and foster parents, is required. In most cases the mixture is working.

8 The Throwaway Kids

AMONG the cruel legacies of the war in Vietnam are the thousands of half-American children left in that country when the U.S. military effort ended there in 1975. They are the children of American servicemen or civilian workers and Vietnamese women. In some cases their fathers were killed in the war. In most cases the fathers simply returned to the United States at the end of their tour of duty and lost all contact with the mothers of their children and with the children themselves. Sometimes they never knew that they left children behind.

In April, 1975, the North Vietnamese government broke a cease-fire agreement, and the Communist Vietcong army moved south. With almost all U.S. military forces gone, the South Vietnamese army fell apart, and within days Communist troops were on the outskirts of Saigon. Panic swept over the South Vietnamese, for no one knew what revenge the forces of Ho Chi Minh would wreak.

Most panic-stricken of all were the mothers of children fathered by Americans. Rumors swept the city and countryside that the mothers would be killed or imprisoned and that the *my lai*, as children of mixed American and Vietnamese blood were called, would also be killed. Some mothers abandoned their children and fled to other towns and cities. Some hid them with grandparents and aunts and uncles in villages. Some tried to disguise their children by staining their faces darker and shaving or dying their hair, but disguise was useless. Some mothers simply kept their children near them and waited for whatever was to happen.

As is often the case, the most terrible rumors were not true. The mothers of children with American fathers were not killed or sent to prison. The children were not killed. But in many cases mothers and children were sent to "New Economic Zones" to work at hard labor for years clearing land, digging irrigation canals, working in fields from morning until night. Housing was poor, food scarce, medical care almost completely lacking. Many mothers and children died of malnutrition, exhaustion, and neglect.

The children themselves, these progeny of American fathers and Vietnamese mothers, have grown up in a climate of scorn and hate. In Vietnam they are called *bui doi*, the "dust of life." *My lai* is a term of ridicule hurled at them constantly. As reminders of a hated enemy or (for many) of bitter defeat, they are considered worthless by most Vietnamese, something to be "thrown away" and forgotten. Many have been put in substandard orphanages. Some survive on city streets, living by their wits, sometimes as part of a gang run by a criminal adult. Even those who have had some semblance of a normal life living with relatives or their mother are frequently discriminated against in school and made fun of by other children.

The existence of as many as fifteen thousand of these half-American children—now generally called Amerasians—has always been well known to the U.S. Defense and State departments and to Congress. For years, however, little was done to try to bring the Amerasian children, or at least some of them, to the United States. It was as if, by ignoring them, the U.S. government could pretend they did not exist.

An Amerasian teen-ager.

In 1979, through the efforts of the U.N. High Commissioner for Refugees, Vietnam established an Orderly Departure Program which enabled some Vietnamese to apply for immigration to other countries. In 1982 Congress finally passed an Amerasian immigration act, which provided support for Amerasian children brought to the United States. Since that date about three thousand Amerasian children have come to America through the Orderly Departure Program.

The first happy cases to enter the United States, relatively few in number, were Amerasian children whose American fathers knew of their existence, knew how they could be located, and signed papers assuming responsibility for them. They entered the country as American citizens and went to live with their fathers. Later, the

State Department authorized the entrance of some Amerasian children with their mothers and other immediate family members even though the fathers were unknown or accepted no responsibility. Now, other Amerasians, some of them orphans or street children, are beginning to come to the United States through the unaccompanied refugee minors program.

In 1984, through the Orderly Departure Program, Truong came to the United States as an unaccompanied minor. He is now living with his foster parents in Maryland. Like most Amerasians, Truong is in his teens—sixteen he thinks, although he is not certain because he has no birth certificate. Truong is tall, has brown hair, and a light brown complexion. The bone structure of his face is American, and it would be hard to pick him out as an Amerasian in any crowd of American teen-agers.

Truong does not remember his American father and is not sure that he ever saw him. He does have shadowy memories of his mother, but he is not certain which are true memories and which are stories told to him by his "grandmother," who raised him in Ho Chi Minh City (the name the victorious North Vietnamese gave to Saigon). The woman was really not his grandmother or in fact any relative. In the panic-filled days before the Communists entered Saigon, Truong's mother left him with the woman. His mother said she was going to get ready to leave the city and would return for him. She never came back, and Truong has no idea what happened to her.

The woman, who was a street vendor of cigarettes and medicine, kept Truong, although she could have taken him to an orphanage. She also found two other young Amerasian boys wandering the Saigon streets, and she took them in. They became Truong's "brothers." Truong went to school, but the other schoolchildren teased him and called him *my lai*; and, Truong recalls, the teacher paid no attention to him. After two years, Truong quit school and helped his foster mother sell cigarettes and medicine. She was very poor, and all three boys worked as street vendors. Because he was big and strong for his age, Truong became a bicycle rickshaw driver when he was thirteen. He made more money that way but not much more because most of what he made went to the man who owned the rickshaw.

When the Orderly Departure Program started, Truong's foster mother found out all the details about it and then told her three boys that she thought they should try to go to America. That was their only chance to have a good life, she said. Truong had never even thought about such a thing, but the idea of living in America excited him, and he said he would go if he could. One of the other boys made the same decision, but the third refused to leave Vietnam and the only mother he had ever known.

Truong arrived at his new home in America without knowing a single word of English. Almost every Amerasian boy and girl arrives the same way. There is no refugee camp to cushion the shock of culture change and to give them a chance to learn some English. They board a plane at Ho Chi Minh City airport one day and one or two days later they are in the United States.

After nine months in America, Truong says he is glad he came, but how well he is adjusting to his new life is not yet clear. He is in school and learning some English but shows little interest in studying. With his poor educational background, he is unlikely to graduate from high school. He knows a good deal about bicycle repair, and his foster parents hope he will go to a trade school and learn other mechanical skills.

There is a large Vietnamese community in the city where Truong lives, and he spends most of his time there. Often he comes in very late at night. His foster parents are disturbed by the hours he keeps, and they tell him the streets are dangerous at night.

"No worry," Truong assures them. "I know streets."

Many people believe that all Vietnamese women who had children by Americans during the war years were bar girls and prostitutes.

That is far from the truth. Of course, children did result from casual encounters with such women, but many mothers of Amerasian children were secretaries, interpreters, bank clerks, businesswomen, and military base workers in different jobs. Their relationships with the men who fathered their children often lasted for several years.

Van, a seventeen-year-old Amerasian boy now living in the United States, remembers his father very well. He worked at a military base in Saigon, and Van's mother worked there also. He thinks she was a cashier at the base cafeteria. They had a little apartment in Saigon, and Van lived there from the time of his earliest memories until the Communists came in 1975, when he was five years old. Van remembers his father as a big, laughing man who played with him and was kind and gentle. He came mainly on weekends, and the three of them would go to movies and on picnics.

Van is not sure, but he thinks it was in 1974 that his father returned to America. His mother was sad, but sometimes letters would come from his father and then she was happy. But the letters stopped coming, and in 1975 the Vietcong overran South Vietnam. Van and his mother never heard from his father again. In her fear of what the Communist conquerors might do, Van's mother burned all letters from his father and all pictures of him, pictures that had been taken in their apartment and on picnics.

Van and his mother were sent to a New Economic Zone, and they labored in the fields there for four years. They worked all day every day, and Van never went to school. After two years his mother became ill and began to lose weight. One morning, after she had been ill for two years, she did not wake up. Van escaped from the New Economic Zone and made his way back to Ho Chi Minh City. He knew that his grandmother and grandfather lived there, and he was able to find them. They kept him for three years and sent him to school; but when the Orderly Departure Program was started, they felt that he should go to the United States.

"I wanted to go," Van says. "I could not wait to go. Every day I asked when I would go. I wanted to find my father. I was sure I could find him once I got to America. I did not know his name because my mother had burned every letter and every piece of paper with his name on it. She had burned every picture, but his face is in my mind clearer than any picture."

Van came to the United States in 1983. He is doing exceptionally well in school and will go to college when he graduates from high school. He has developed an affectionate relationship with his foster parents, but the idea of finding his real father remains very much in his mind.

"Someday I will find him," says Van, "and he will be happy to see me."

Kim is a fifteen-year-old Amerasian girl who has been in America less than a year. She does not remember her father or her mother, who left her with an aunt and an uncle when she was an infant. The aunt and uncle had a large family of their own, and the presence of a half-American child was a burden and an embarrassment. When they learned of the Orderly Departure Program, they insisted that Kim go to America.

Kim was terrified at the idea of going to a strange country alone and begged to stay with them, but they pushed ahead with getting her departure papers. When she said that she would not go, they threatened to put her out on the street or to send her to a children's home (orphanage). Finally, she went.

Kim's first nine months in America have been a disaster. She has been in three different foster homes. She is depressed, sullen, unwilling to make any effort at school or in the home. She has threatened suicide more than once.

"I don't know what will become of her," says her social worker. "We have to find the key that will make her want to try."

Perhaps it has now been found. Kim is in her fourth foster home, a large Vietnamese family that came to America as refugees

Art therapy drawing by a young Amerasian girl, not showing her face.

in 1975. They can offer her the security of familiar language and customs and at the same time ease her into life in America. For the first time Kim is showing signs of emerging from her depression.

Most Amerasian children have not had a real childhood. They have spent many of their young years helping their caretakers earn a living. They have toiled at forced labor in New Economic Zones. They have been locked away in dreary orphanages. They have been scorned and excluded from play by other children.

Among the most deprived of Amerasian children are those who have lived much of their lives in orphanages. Sister Marilyn Lacey, in her excellent study of Amerasian children in America, *In Their Fathers' Land*, reports that caseworkers have found unaccompanied refugee minors who came from orphanages in Vietnam ". . . lacked nurturance and care, had little education, and craved attention." She further reports that those from orphanages are frequently so under-sized physically that they give the appearance of being several years younger than they actually are.

Hung, an Amerasian boy who was raised in an orphanage near Ho Chi Minh City, came to America in 1984 through the Orderly Departure Program. There was some question about his age, but his size seemed to suggest that he was no more than twelve years old, and his foster parents were told that was his probable age. Amerasian children who come from orphanages frequently have a hard time learning how to live as a part of a family, but Hung did not have that problem. He loved to be with his foster parents and to play with his foster brother and sister, both of whom were younger than Hung. He was fascinated by stuffed animals, me-chanical toys, and bright-colored picture books, and his room was soon full of those trappings of childhood that had never been a part of his life in Vietnam. Hung responded to a diet of good, nutritious food, and he learned English quickly.

After Hung had been in his new home about six months, a reexamination of his records, additional information received, and reports from his teachers and counselors raised the possibility that he might be older than twelve, perhaps as old as fifteen. Somehow Hung learned of this question about his age, and he was quite disturbed. After two or three days of silence that was not at all like him, he burst out crying one morning and said to his foster mother, "Do I have to be fifteen?"

The wise decision was that he did not. There would be time to explore his age again after he had caught up on some of his lost childhood.

Who am I? The question is a serious one for most Amerasians. In Vietnam, they are reminded every day that they are *my lai*, someone of mixed blood, a half-breed. Furthermore, in Vietnamese culture a person's identity is always linked to his father, so to be without a

Many unaccompanied refugees have lost childhood to catch up on. This Vietnamese boy (not an Amerasian) has found a friend.

father and to know nothing about him is a constant source of confusion and shame.

In Their Fathers' Land reports that problems of self-identity continue for Amerasians when they come to the United States. A survey shows that 40 percent think of themselves as Amerasians (both Vietnamese and American), 25 percent consider themselves Vietnamese, and only 15 percent think of themselves as being Americans, even though they have American fathers and are now living in America. (Twenty percent of the cases surveyed did not

Lisa.

clearly answer the question about self-identity). The report notes that a higher percentage of Amerasians with black fathers thought of themselves as Americans than those with white fathers; no reason is given for this difference.

Lisa is an Amerasian girl of eighteen whose father was black. She knows nothing about him but hopes someday to find him. "I dreamed of coming to my father's country," she says, and two years ago she did, through the Orderly Departure Program.

When questioned about how she thinks of herself, Lisa responds

The Nunn family.

very logically, "When I am with Vietnamese, I feel Vietnamese. When I am with Americans, I feel American."

But clearly Lisa is becoming more and more American. Since she has been in the United States she has had the very good fortune of being in the foster care of Betsy and Walter Nunn, a warm, perceptive couple who live in Falls Church, Virginia. The Nunns have two adopted American children, and, in addition to Lisa, they are foster parents to a Vietnamese boy and girl. Betsy Nunn is a teacher of data processing in Falls Church schools, and Walter is a U.S. Navy analyst.

In this well-integrated, well-guided family Lisa has gained confidence in getting along with other teen-agers and has been encouraged to make her own decisions about life. Her decision to become "Lisa" rather than to retain her Vietnamese name Tho was entirely her own.

"Kids in school made fun of my name and couldn't say it right," she explains, "so I changed it to Lisa. I like the way it sounds."

Lisa's life has quickly grown into a full and busy one. She is a sophomore in high school, sings in the church choir, and is now working part-time at a nearby Kentucky Fried Chicken. After she graduates from high school, she wants to become a nurse.

Mrs. Nunn thinks that scholarship funds may be available to help Lisa with the costs of nurse's training, but she says that she and her husband will support Lisa through her education after high school if necessary. "Somehow we will find a way," she says. "We think of Lisa as our daughter."

Lisa's reason for wanting to be a nurse is clear and simple. "I want to help people," she says.

Sister Marilyn's study reveals important and sometimes surprising information about unaccompanied Amerasian minors. Despite their hard life in Vietnam, a disturbing 22 percent say that they did not want to come to America. By contrast, only 1 percent of Amerasians who came with their mothers and other family members say that they came against their will. This is clear evidence that the fear of being plunged alone into an unknown land is overwhelming to many. Although the decision for them to leave Vietnam may be in their long-term best interest, the beginning of the experience is terrifying to a large number.

Over half of all unaccompanied Amerasian minors in the study (55 percent) say that they know nothing about their American fathers. Only 17 percent have any hopes that they may someday be reunited with their fathers, and over half never mention the subject or do *not* want to be with their fathers. A much higher percentage of Amerasian children in the United States with their mothers know something about their fathers and would like to be reunited with them.

But sometimes the desire of Amerasian children to find their fathers is intense. Sister Marilyn quotes one fifteen-year-old Amerasian girl who has never seen her father and does not even know his name: "I'm always watching on the streets. Maybe that way someday I'll see him. His face will be my face."

9 Being a Foster Parent: Hard but Worth Doing

I N MOST cities with programs for unaccompanied refugee minors, foster parents meet once a month with the program director or a caseworker to talk about problems and to share experiences, information, and ideas. Whenever we met with these support groups, we always asked the same question:

"Why did you become foster parents?"

At one meeting a foster mother responded quickly: "Because we didn't know how hard it was going to be."

Everyone laughed, but no one argued that being a foster parent is easy. Every foster parent goes through many of the same frustrations, anxieties, and fears that the refugee child or teen-ager experiences. The foster parents want to talk to their new foster son or daughter but can't except in the most limited way. They want to serve food that he likes, but he seems to like almost nothing. They want to know about his past life but can find out little. He is in the house but not really a part of the family.

Almost without exception foster parents look forward to a close and caring relationship with their refugee foster son or daughter, and they hope that this new young person in their lives will form an affectionate attachment to them. They hope there will be a bonding that will last into the future.

Such bonding does take place but by no means always. Sometimes the young refugees remain withdrawn, unresponsive, homesick, or angry. They are clearly unhappy, and they do not seem to try to fit into their new family. The foster parents cannot establish a link of affection with their foster child, and this failure is disappointing and painful.

"Some of these children will be bleeding emotionally for a long time," says Dr. Lee in explaining this kind of behavior.

Sometimes the emotional problems of the unaccompanied refugee minors are severe, particularly for the younger ones who are less able to understand why they have been separated from their families. In one case of ten- and fourteen-year-old brothers, the younger brother had uncontrollable fits of rage. His behavior so upset the older brother that he stayed in his room almost all the time. After five months the foster parents gave up and asked for the boys to be transferred someplace else.

The young boy's chaotic behavior and the older brother's withdrawal continued in their second foster home. Many times in the first months the new foster parents wanted to return the boys to the refugee agency. But this husband and wife had been through a severe drug problem with one of their natural sons a few years earlier. Terrible emotional stress and strain were nothing new to them, and they stuck with their commitment to their refugee foster sons. Slowly, as the younger boy developed affection for this foster father, his wild temper began to subside. As that happened, the older brother came out of his protective shell and became a well-adjusted boy; he made a number of friends and won a place on the school soccer team. These foster parents clearly were the right ones for this difficult case.

Bonding between the foster father and the boy was important in this instance. Child psychologists in the refugee program point out, however, that program objectives usually can be reached without bonding taking place.

"Foster parents have to provide food and shelter," says one unaccompanied refugee minor program director. "They have to provide a stable home environment. They have to help their foster child develop some independence and what we call life skills—getting along with people, handling money, taking care of his room and his clothes.

"If they can make him happy, too, that's wonderful, but it's an extra. Does that sound hardhearted? It's not. It's realistic, and knowing what the real objectives are is the only way some foster parents can keep going. Even so, we have a breakdown in about one out of every five placements and have to find new foster homes for the kids."

Yet for every story of pain, disappointment, or "just getting along," there is a story of the satisfactions and sometimes warmth that can and do come out of the relationship between foster parents and their refugee foster children. We heard and saw the good stories everywhere.

Marshall and Dorothy Sherman live in McLean, Virginia, a Washington, D.C., suburb, with their three daughters: Kathryn and Kristen, thirteen-year-old twins, and Ginger, who is six. Marshall Sherman is a captain in the U.S. Navy, assigned to the Pentagon. Dorothy Sherman teaches learning disabled students at a McLean high school. With three lively daughters and very full professional lives the Shermans would seem to have more than enough to keep them busy, yet for the past 2½ years they have been foster parents to five unaccompanied refugee minors.

Three of the boys have moved on, two having reached the emancipation age of eighteen, one, a Vietnamese, to live with a Vietnamese family. But two remain: nineteen-year-old Mario from El Salvador and Tilahun, a sixteen-year-old Ethiopian boy. Mario has been with the Shermans for eighteen months and, although he is nineteen now, he will stay with them until he graduates from high school in another year's time. Tilahun, who made a daring escape from Ethiopia by stowing away on a merchant ship, has been in the Sherman's foster care for a year.

Both Mario and Tilahun came to the Shermans from breakdowns with other foster families. Fitting these two teen-age boys from totally different cultures into the Sherman family life has been far from easy, but everyone has had a part in making this second try work. No one wanted another breakdown.

For a long time Mario refused to make what Dorothy Sherman calls "a human connection." Even though he learned English quickly, he communicated very little with the family, prized his independence, and spent much of his time outside the home. Mario's past, insofar as it can be pieced together, makes these characteristics more understandable. He says that one of his brothers was killed by the El Salvadoran army and that he, Mario, left home in fear of the army when he was eleven years old. He spent four years in the hills and jungles of El Salvador with antigovernment forces, hunted the whole time by the army. In a rare move, the El Salvadoran government allowed a group of antigovernment people, including Mario, to leave the country, and the United States gave them political asylum. Only then was the discovery made that Mario was a minor, which made him eligible for the unaccompanied refugee minors program.

Patience was the answer in Mario's case, and the Shermans had patience. If he was late for meals or didn't show up at all, his absence was not treated as a family crisis. When there were difficulties at school, as there were, Dorothy Sherman, experienced in such troubles, helped quietly. Marshall Sherman is himself a reserved man, which in his relationship with Mario was good because Mario did not feel pressured. But Marshall takes satisfaction in the progress of the young adults who have been in his and his wife's care. He was always available if Mario wanted to talk and to provide help with schoolwork when help was needed.

The Shermans with Mario and Tilahun and the rest of their family.

The turnaround, when it came, was sudden and complete. On New Year's Day, when Mario had been with the Shermans for almost exactly a year, he told everyone in the family how much they meant to him and how important they were to him. The macho, independent, silent young man suddenly could talk. He could tell people how he felt.

"Now Mario and I can talk about anything," Dorothy Sherman says. "He still has some school problems, and we discuss them. He even tells me about his girl friends!"

More and more Mario wants to spend all of the time he is not in school with his foster family. Dorothy has some doubts about this, feeling that perhaps he should be doing more things outside. But the psychologist in the unaccompanied refugee minors program says she should not worry.

"Mario is making up for some of the home and family life he missed in El Salvador," he says. "It's a good thing."

Tilahun lived in the Ethiopian port city of Assab. He made his dangerous escape by swimming to a ship anchored offshore and climbing the anchor chain. He left Ethiopia because he hated the Marxist army and hated even more the certainty of having to serve in it when he reached the age of sixteen. Tilahun did not get along well with the children in his first foster home in America, but he has had no trouble in the Sherman home.

"In fact," says Dorothy, "the first real breakthrough of close feelings came between Tilahun and Ginger. The same was true of Mario. Both boys play with her. I guess it's easier to express how you feel with the youngest one."

All three girls helped Tilahun and Mario with their English, and good feeling among them exists all around. "They're just like brothers to me now," says Kathryn and adds that was not true of the others who have been in foster care in their house.

Tilahun is a serious boy. He studies hard and makes good grades in school. He also works two hours a day at a nearby McDonald's and sends part of what he earns to his family in Ethiopia. Although there is no strain between Tilahun and his foster mother, he communicates more easily with Marshall Sherman.

"I think that is cultural," Dorothy says, "the way it would be in Ethiopia. I don't worry about it."

Dorothy Sherman knows very clearly why she has invested so much time in being a foster parent. "I like kids," she says. "I have good parenting skills, and I like to use them."

Recently Dorothy talked with a group of soon-to-be foster parents in one of the training sessions held to help them get ready for their new responsibilities. "I told them not to expect the kids to be grateful," she says. "They don't know what to expect when they arrive. They just take whatever is given to them. I think the ones who have been here a long time know how much has been done for them.

"And," Dorothy Sherman continues, "I told them not to expect a close relationship with their foster children. It may happen and it may not. But they can do a good job without it happening. I told them to remember that and to take satisfaction in doing a good job."

Huong and Thieu Dao are a young Vietnamese couple who live in Springfield, Virginia. Only a year ago they had no children. Today they have five. "We wanted one little girl," says Huong Dao with a smile. "Now we have three boys and two girls, and all are teen-agers or almost teen-agers."

The Daos are one of hundreds of Vietnamese, Cambodian, and Laotian families in the United States who have become foster parents to unaccompanied refugee youth. The Catholic and Lutheran agencies would like to recruit more ethnic foster parents, but they are not easy to find. Most Southeast Asians who have come to America in the last decade are busy making a place for themselves in their new country. They do not have time or room in their homes for foster children. Still, about 10 percent of all unaccompanied young refugees are now living with foster parents of their own nationality.

The Daos volunteered as foster parents because, without children of their own, they were lonely and felt they had love to give. They were also convinced that Vietnamese who were now well settled in America should help in giving care to young unaccompanied refugees from their country.

Mr. and Mrs. Dao came to the United States in the first wave of refugees from Vietnam in 1975. Mr. Dao was a South Vietnamese government official and would have been a marked man on the Communist retaliation list. In America, Mr. Dao worked as a janitor at the University of Iowa and studied mechanical engineering there.

The Dao foster children.

Today he is a computer hardware specialist, and Mrs. Dao is a dental assistant. They both have become U.S. citizens.

With their decision to become foster parents made, the Daos asked Connections, the Catholic-related placement agency in their area, for a young girl. None was available, but a foster home was needed for Dinh, a fifteen-year-old Vietnamese boy who was soon to arrive after a year in a Thailand refugee camp. The Daos agreed to take him.

Dinh did arrive and became Huong and Thieu Dao's first foster child. Their house in Springfield is large and comfortable, and in the months that followed it has steadily filled up with other young Vietnamese refugees. Their experience with Dinh was going so well that Connections asked the Daos if they would take Tai, a seventeen-year-old boy who needed a change from the home he was in at that time. The Daos agreed to take him on a temporary basis while another home was sought for him, but after a short time they decided there was no reason why Tai should not stay with them. Then came Lam, a lively twelve-year-old boy who tried three times before succeeding in his escape from Vietnam. Finally, the Daos were asked, and agreed, to become foster parents to two Amerasian girls, Phuong, twelve, and Bong, fifteen.

Isn't this an overload for a young couple without any experience as parents? "No," says Mr. Dao, "but it is a load."

He points out that he and his wife have the tremendous advantage of being able to speak to their foster children in their own language and in knowing and understanding completely their customs. And they have a firsthand understanding of the fear, confusion, and uncertainty that the young refugees in their care have experienced and are still experiencing. After escaping from Vietnam, the Daos spent several months in a camp on Guam where refugees were held and additional time at a refugee processing center in Florida. The Daos offer their foster children an ideal example of two Vietnamese who arrived penniless in America and succeeded through study and hard work.

If Connections officials had one concern, it was that the Daos might not be entirely sure-handed in bringing discipline and organization to their large new family. But that concern has proved to be unfounded. Each of the five foster children has his or her own set of household chores to accomplish, including keeping their rooms in good order and taking turns in the kitchen, cleaning and chopping vegetables for the Vietnamese dishes that fill the dining room table every night. Everyone is expected to be home by dark, and homework is a nighttime priority activity in which Mr. Dao takes a close supervisory interest. But there is time for relaxation, too. The Daos

Lam playing on the new cabin cruiser.

have recently bought a handsome eighteen-foot cabin cruiser, and on weekends the family spends much of their time on the Potomac River and in the waters around Annapolis.

Would the Daos like to expand their foster family still more? Huong Dao smiles. "Five is enough," she says.

Sierra Vista is an attractive small city in southern Arizona just twenty miles from the Mexican border. Nearby Fort Huacuca, whose cavalry troops once fought battles with the Apaches, is the oldest active military base in the country. Sierra Vista's size and good schools, strong in English as a Second Language, make it an excellent location for the small group of unaccompanied refugee teen-agers who live in foster homes there.

Jack and Karen Devine live in Sierra Vista with their fifteen-year-old daughter, Danielle. For over a year the Devines have been foster parents to two Vietnamese brothers, Thoai (pronounced Toy), sixteen, and Bao, fifteen. Jack Devine, who has a doctorate in education, is assistant principal at Buena High School. Karen teaches at Town and Country Elementary School and has taught English as a Second Language.

The day we visited the Devines in Sierra Vista, we began, as we usually did, with the question of why. Why would a family that is getting along well, nice house, no unusual problems, decide to disrupt their lives by taking in a total stranger, not just for a few days or weeks but possibly for years? And not just a stranger but a stranger from a strange country, a stranger with incomprehensible language and customs that they knew nothing about.

"Why did you decide to do it?" we asked.

"Jack and I were Peace Corps volunteers in the sixties," Karen told us. "He was in Africa; I was in South America. So different languages and different customs are nothing new to us. We heard about the foster parent program for refugee children, and it made sense to us."

Jack added his thoughts. "Our country's whole Vietnam experience was a troubling one. Helping a Vietnamese child seemed right somehow."

"And you ended up helping two teen-age boys."

"That wasn't what we had in mind when we volunteered," Karen said. "We agreed to take one, and Thoai was sent to us."

Karen described Thoai's entrance into the family as one with no unusual problems. He was a quiet, deeply religious boy. He plunged into his studies at school and built a small shrine above his bed in his room. It is a small platform attached to the wall. On it are a ceramic image of the Buddha, candles, incense, and a little vase for fresh flowers whenever Thoai can get them. Every morning,

Thoai (in dark sweater) and Bao with their foster parents.

Karen told us, he puts on a white robe and prays in front of the shrine.

Bit by bit, as Thoai learned English, he told Jack, Karen, and Danielle about his family and their life in Vietnam. He had three brothers: Bao, fourteen (at that time), Vinh, twelve, and Duy, eleven. Bao had escaped from Vietnam after Thoai and was then in a refugee camp in Indonesia. Vinh and Duy were still in Vietnam.

Thoai's mother had died five years ago. He had an aunt who was a Buddhist nun. Before the Communist victory in Vietnam, Thoai's father had been a successful businessman in the transportation business with trucks and buses. After the Communist takeover, he had lost his business and had been put in prison. After his release, he found a job as a bus driver, and in that way provided a living for his family.

Thoai, like so many other young Vietnamese refugees, had no inkling that he was about to be separated from his family and sent on a perilous journey to a refugee camp. One night his father took him on a bus to another town, put him on a boat, and he was gone from Vietnam. After six months in a Malaysian refugee camp, he had come to America and into the Devines' lives.

Thoai established letter contact with his father and Buddhist nun aunt; his aunt now sends him instructions on proper Buddhist behavior. In the best Peace Corps tradition, Karen taught herself to write Vietnamese script and began corresponding with Thoai's father and aunt, giving them a good foster parental account of how Thoai was adjusting to his new life.

"Then," Karen said, "we learned that Bao's papers had been processed in the Indonesian refugee camp and that he was ready to come to a foster home in America. We were asked if we could take him. I guess that was inevitable."

Jack, Karen, and Danielle talked over the possibility of further increasing their family and found the decision surprisingly easy to make. Thoai was such a quiet, serious boy that they sometimes hardly knew he was in the house. There had been some problems with meals since Thoai didn't eat meat, but they had not been hard to solve; and he had learned to love pizza so much that Karen had to ration it. The family agreed there was no reason why Bao should not come to live with them and share Thoai's room.

Vietnamese brothers, the Devines soon learned, can be just as different as American brothers. Bao literally burst upon the scene. He was talkative, made friends easily, was curious and inquisitive about everything around him, a real live wire. He had learned quite a bit of English in the refugee camp and had established many friendships there. He soon began to receive letters from former camp friends now in the United States and in other parts of the world. He sent out his answers, and a national-international correspondence was established.

Karen remembered the first snowfall in Sierra Vista, after both

Thoai and Bao were there. Neither had ever seen snow before, but their reactions to it were quite different. Thoai took one look out the window and went back to bed, pulling the covers over his head. Bao jumped up, dressed quickly, and dashed outside. Soon he was in a snowball fight with Jack, Karen, Danielle, and the neighbors.

The beauty of the snow finally brought Thoai outside, but he was horrified at the snowball fight. No amount of coaxing could get him to join the fun. The idea of family and friends pelting each other with icy missiles was totally alien to his Buddhist precepts.

Yet Thoai goes to karate classes two nights a week and is very much into weight lifting and other physical fitness routines. All this activity is consistent with his religious principles of proper care of the body.

Sometimes Thoai will stop talking for several days at a time. He doesn't seem depressed, just silent. Karen and Jack think the silence has something to do with Thoai's religion, but they aren't sure and it worries them. But Bao tells them, "Don't worry. He won't talk to me either." In a few days Thoai will begin talking as if he had never stopped.

Once Jack and Karen drove Thoai and Bao to Phoenix to see a monk at the Buddhist temple there. Thoai had looked forward to discussing Buddhist philosophy with the holy man, but he came away disappointed. "He just talked about how important it is for us to learn English," Thoai said.

Although they are a year apart in age, Thoai and Bao are both in the ninth grade, and both are good and serious students. Each has made the school honor roll this year, and they both have been accepted for the honors program next year. Their courses will include English, mathematics, chemistry, and geography. They dutifully report their academic progress to their father in Vietnam, and he is pleased.

Danielle and the boys get along well, but they are not particularly close. Danielle's routines with friends, school, and social activities were set long before Thoai and Bao became a part of the family,

and even though the three are close together in age, there has been little interaction outside the home. Thoai and Bao tend to spend their free time with their Vietnamese friends. This is a pattern we observed everyplace we went. The barriers of culture and language are high, and only time will lower them.

We were surprised to learn that Vinh, Thoai and Bao's younger brother, was now living in Sierra Vista. He had escaped from Vietnam after Bao and spent time in a refugee camp. The Devines were unable to take Vinh because there was no more room in their house, but other foster parents were found for him in Sierra Vista so that the brothers could be together. (We heard months later that the fourth brother, Duy, has escaped and is in a refugee camp in Malaysia. When he, too, arrives in Sierra Vista, as he almost certainly will, the father's great task of getting his four sons to freedom will be finished.)

College is very much in Thoai and Bao's future plans, and Jack and Karen are helping them look down the road. They have set up bank accounts for the boys and encourage them to put in some of their allowance, as well as money they make from occasional odd jobs. Thoai is planning to work as a busboy in a restaurant during the summer and to bank his earnings. Bao has no such summer job planned. He enjoys playing golf with Jack and intends to take lessons during the summer so that he can give his foster father a better game.

"But," Karen said, "Bao is going to take a summer ESL course."

Jack summed up their experience as foster parents to two very different Vietnamese boys. "Thoai and Bao are a part of this family," he said. "They will always be a part of it."

That night the foster parents of Vietnamese refugee boys in Sierra Vista held a pot luck supper at the home of Agnes and Jay Raschke. The occasion was a visit from Dr. Daniel Lee, the Vietnamese psychologist, and all the young refugees had gathered after school for a long group counseling session with him. After the session they were relaxed and very hungry, loading their plates with huge portions of Vietnamese chicken salad, lasagna, rice, and desserts. After eating, they got into a lively card game, and it seemed to us that the gathering might have been one of teen-agers and their parents anywhere in America.

We met the Raschkes' foster son, Cuong, whom Agnes introduced with obvious affection as "my preppy Vietnamese," explaining that he was particularly fussy about his haircuts and his clothes.

Teen-age unaccompanied refugees in Sierra Vista, Arizona.

But Cuong, we learned, has a serious side. He is the only son in his family and has four younger sisters in Vietnam. The family is poor, and Cuong sends them packages of clothes and other goods. Agnes says the packages are taxed in Vietnam but still very much worth receiving.

So that he could send his family more, Cuong worked the previous summer for the Sierra Vista Parks Department. He had to interview for the job and was afraid he wouldn't have the right answers.

"You passed your immigration interview in the refugee camp," Agnes told him. "You can pass a Parks Department interview."

The Parks Department interviewer, as the episode was reported to Agnes, did not make the session easy for Cuong. "You don't look

Agnes Raschke with her foster son, Cuong.

Relaxing after a counseling session.

very strong," he said to Cuong. "Do you think you can do this hard work?"

Cuong was caught by the police in his first escape attempt from Vietnam. "I did hard work for a year in a labor camp in Vietnam," he told the interviewer.

"Do you think you can follow orders?" the interviewer asked.

"Yes," Cuong said. "I followed orders in the labor camp." And then he added, "The guards had guns."

Cuong got the job.

During the evening at the Raschkes, the foster parents chatted, compared experiences, and took advantage of Dr. Lee's presence to ask him questions and go over any problems they had. One foster mother was concerned that her foster son had a great appetite for reading kung fu novels written in Vietnamese; she wasn't sure where he got them.

"Does reading them keep him from doing his schoolwork?" Dr. Lee asked.

"No," the foster mother said.

"Let him read," Dr. Lee told her.

At one point during the evening, Jay Raschke looked around his living room at his guests and said to us, "One of the nice bonuses of being a foster parent is that we have gotten to know such fine people."

From having seen a number of such groups, we could fully understand Jay's feelings.

10 | Group Homes

I T IS Tuesday night, and there is a flurry of activity inside the brick house on Pritchard Street in Wheaton, Maryland. The house looks like hundreds of other single-family homes in the area, but the people who live in it make it quite different.

Alan, a sixteen-year-old Cambodian boy, is vacuuming the living room. Leng, his older brother, has dusted the first floor and is working his way into the basement. Fifteen-year-old Tesfi, from Eritrea, is in the kitchen chopping onions for his spaghetti sauce. Chung, from Vietnam, is scouring the tiles in the bathroom.

The front door opens and Chung's brother, Tuan, walks in carrying two heavy bags of groceries. He is followed by Gil, a tall American man, with a similar load. "We need some help with the groceries," Gil says. "Alan, can you give us a hand?"

Alan turns off the vacuum and goes outside to help. Tuan carries his load into the kitchen, takes one look at the pots on the stove and says, "Spaghetti again. Every time Tesfi cooks is spaghetti. All the time spaghetti."

"I like spaghetti," says Tesfi, standing proudly over his pots.

Tesfi cooking.

Elspeth, Gil's wife, comes into the kitchen. "What are you serving with it?" she asks.

"Corn," Tesfi tells her. "I like corn."

"Don't you think we should have a green vegetable? Some salad or broccoli perhaps?" Elspeth asks. "Remember the four food groups. Spaghetti and corn are in the same group."

Leng, Alan, Chung, Tuan, and Tesfi, five bright young men from three different countries, are unaccompanied refugee minors living in one of three group homes established by Associated Catholic Charities in this Maryland suburb of Washington, D.C. Gil and Elspeth Schwenk are their house parents.

Refugee agencies placing unaccompanied refugee minors sometimes use group homes such as this one on Pritchard Street to provide foster care, instead of using foster parents. The group homes are supervised by house parents, who are employed by the sponsoring Catholic or Lutheran organization. Young refugees—usually from four to six in a home—who are placed in this kind of foster care are almost always older teen-age boys who have been on their own in their home countries or in refugee camps for so long that they are too independent to fit easily into the family life of foster parents.

That is the case for Leng and Alan, the Cambodian brothers, and for Chung and Tuan, Vietnamese brothers, who are all in their late teens and in high school. Only Tesfi is an exception. He is from Eritrea, a northern province of Ethiopia that has been trying for decades to win its independence. When he was only eight years old, Tesfi was taken from his parents by rebel troops and placed in a camp where he received military training, including rifle marksmanship and hand-to-hand fighting with knives.

Tesfi was in the camp for four years before he and an older friend had a chance to escape. They made their way to a port city, stowed away on a ship, and eventually landed in the United States, where they were given refugee status. Even though he was only twelve, Tesfi was put into the Pritchard Street group home because there was no suitable foster home for him at the time. By the time

Celebrating Cambodian New Year at the Pritchard Street group home. Elspeth, Chung, and Leng with guests.

a foster family was found, he had adjusted to the group home and did not want to leave. He has now been at the home longer than any of the other boys there, longer, too, than Elspeth and Gil.

Elspeth and Gil Schwenk have been house parents in the Pritchard Street group home for about a year. Like the majority of house parents, they are a young couple who have no children of their own, but they compensate for the lack of experience as parents by having backgrounds that are useful in living with and supervising the young refugees. Elspeth has a master's degree in clinical psychology, and Gil works during the day for a Washington, D.C., refugee organization.

For the boys, day-to-day life in the Pritchard Street home is

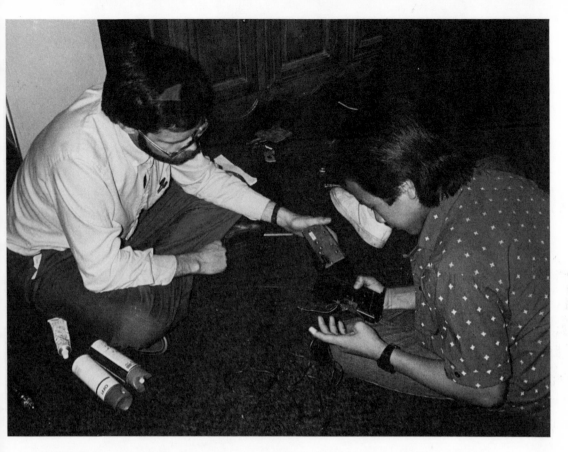

Gil Schwenk, group home house parent, teaches Tuan how to repair a tape recorder.

not too different from what it would be in a foster home. They are off to school each day and either work at part-time jobs or play soccer after school and on weekends. If they want to go out at night, they get permission from one of their house parents. Elspeth and Gil encourage study, help with homework, and arbitrate any disputes that arise. Sometimes they take the boys on weekend trips to the beach.

The most important house rule is that each person must respect the rights of the others. "Whenever we have a conflict, we use that rule to settle it," Elspeth says, "and it seems to work."

Life in a group home can give the young refugee good preparation for the time he will be on his own. In foster homes, the foster

Elspeth and Leng shopping.

mother frequently does all of the cooking and clothes washing and most of the house cleaning. In the group home, household chores are divided up, each person being assigned a different responsibility every week. In this way they all learn to cook, clean house, wash clothes, and shop for groceries. Some of the boys, who have never done anything of this kind in their lives, object at first, but they learn soon enough that such activity is a part of their new life.

Elspeth or Gil and one of the boys make a shopping list and go to the supermarket once a week. Since each person in the house—including the Schwenks—is responsible for cooking dinner once a week, everyone contributes to the list the items he will need for his meal. Elspeth adds breakfast items and snacks such as fruit and cookies.

Dinner at the Pritchard Street group home.

The boys have found that there is much to learn on the shopping expeditions. They have to distinguish between different types of milk and cheese and many other kinds of food products. They must learn to buy within the food budget. This means learning to shop for bargains, to read unit pricing labels, and sometimes to substitute items on the shopping list. Elspeth and Gil have discovered that teaching one section of the supermarket at a time works best.

The relationships that young refugees form in group homes are likely to be more transitory than those formed in foster families. Boys leave the group homes when they graduate from high school and others replace them. House parents, too, tend to move on after a year or two of the demanding work. The Schwenks will soon be leaving the Pritchard Street home for jobs in England.

"It is hard to leave," Elspeth says. "We have grown very fond of these boys in the year we've been here. I hope we can keep in touch with them and see them again, but who can say?"

The boys feel the separation, too, but separations have become a part of their lives.

11 Emancipation: End and Beginning

PHAN is twenty-two, a thoughtful young man who has now been "emancipated" from the unaccompanied refugee minors program for two years. Before emancipation, he lived with his foster parents in northern Virginia from the time he entered the United States at age fifteen until he graduated from high school at age twenty. Now he lives with a Vietnamese family in a large Vietnamese urban community near Washington, D.C.

"I looked it up," Phan said, speaking of the word emancipation, "so many times. It means to be set free. I knew I would be emancipated when I finished high school. Sometimes I thought, why do I have to be set free? Why can't I keep living with Mom and Dad? And then I would think, yes, I want to be set free and live by myself and get a good job and make lots of money. And then the next day I would not be sure what I wanted."

In his mixed and conflicting feelings, Phan was very much like hundreds of unaccompanied refugee youth who have reached the legal age of separation from the program of government financial support and supervision. One of the meanings of emancipation is,

as Phan said, to be set free, but the legal meaning, as it is used in
the unaccompanied refugee minors program is to release a child
from parental control or supervision. The legal age of emancipation
from foster care in most states is eighteen, though in some, support
can continue until the age of twenty-one if the refugee youth is still
completing high school.

Reasons for conflicting feelings about emancipation are easy to
understand. Most young people, as they grow into their teens, want
more independence. They want to try new things, to have less
parental restraint. In this desire for greater freedom, refugee youth
are no different from anyone else, but there is an important difference.

Refugees who entered America as unaccompanied minors have
lived lives of great uncertainty. Their family life in their home
countries was probably disrupted by war and political violence.
Being sent out of the country alone was a separation of great trauma.
They learned to live in refugee camps, made friends, and then they
were sent to America. In time, most adjusted to foster family life
in America, and many developed true affection for their foster
parents. Then within a few years, they are faced with emancipation—
another separation, another beginning.

The staffs of the unaccompanied refugee minors programs are
constantly aware that the day of emancipation is coming for the
refugee youth, in many cases before they are really ready for it.
They also know that the young refugee's best chance to have a
successful life after emancipation is to have a good education, a
reasonable command of English, and a foundation of "life skills"—
the ability to make decisions, to get along with people, to manage
money, to have some knowledge of household responsibilities. Foster
parents are encouraged from the first day to help their refugee foster
children achieve those skills.

Like many foster parents, Phan's foster mother and father told
him he could continue to live with them until he found a job or
decided to go to college. He did stay with them for several months,

but when he got a job in a restaurant in downtown Washington, he moved in with the Vietnamese family of a school friend of his.

A large number of emancipated refugee youth live with families of their own nationality. In Vietnam, Cambodia, and Laos, families are large and family support is a deeply ingrained way of life. Young refugees who come to America alone do not have that support, and many seek it by living with families of their countrymen. It is not the same thing as having one's own family, but the familiarity of language, customs, and culture do provide support when the young refugee begins life on his own in what is still, in many ways, a strange country.

In many cases, emancipated young refugees choose to live with relatives already in America: aunts, uncles, cousins, sometimes brothers and sisters. Living with them before emancipation was not possible because supervision, finances, and housing would not meet the standards required by welfare agencies for foster care. But after the young refugee is older, has made some adjustment to the country, and is able to work, this family reunification does become possible.

The ultimate family reunification—bringing their father, mother, sisters, brothers to America through the Orderly Departure Program—is the ambition of probably 90 percent of all emancipated Vietnamese youth. To have even a chance of making that dream come true, they must become successful, save money, and have a home so that they can sponsor their family still in Vietnam. The number who finally succeed in getting their families out of Vietnam may not be great, but the hope alone provides a powerful motive to get an education and a good job.

The fact that most emancipated refugee youth are living with ethnic families does not mean that they are pulling away from association with Americans. A study by the U.S. Catholic Conference showed that 65 percent of emancipated refugees reported having American friends. Most maintained a relationship with their foster parents, and many found that it was easier to make American friends

in college and on the job than in high school. The majority of
refugee youth, once on their own, do truly begin to live in two
cultural worlds: the culture of their homeland and the dominant
American culture. In this regard, they are not unlike millions of
immigrants who have come to this country in decades past.

Other findings of the USCC study of emancipated refugee
youth are encouraging. Eighty percent are working, the majority in
blue collar activities: restaurants, construction, custodial. Many of
those holding such jobs are working part-time while continuing their
education in college, trade schools, or finishing high school. Almost
20 percent are working in offices and 10 percent are employed in
the field of electronics.

Seventy percent of young emancipated refugees are still in some
kind of school, either full-time or part-time, and a surprising 40
percent are studying at the college level. The majority of those in
college hope for careers in science or engineering, but a large number
are interested in business and industry.

Nguu Bach Thi is an emancipated refugee in his early twenties.
In some ways he is like most young unaccompanied refugees; in
other ways he is special and different. He is the same in that he
escaped from Vietnam because he saw no chance of getting a good
education there. His father, a construction engineer, was in disfavor
with the Communist government, although he was not actually
persecuted. Nguu left a large family in Vietnam; a younger brother
and an older sister also have escaped from Vietnam and come to
America since Nguu arrived, but a second sister was caught trying
to escape and is in jail at this time. Nguu hopes that someday he
can help other members of his family come to the United States.

Nguu is special in that, once enrolled in a Maryland high school,
he discovered a talent for art and graphic design, a talent he had
never been aware of in Vietnam. His high school teachers worked
diligently with Nguu to develop his natural abilities, and his progress
can only be called astonishing. In the academic years 1983 and 1984
he won first, second, or third prizes in twelve different art contests

Nguu Bach Thi, one of the many unaccompanied refugees who has made the successful transition to life in the United States, holds one of his award-winning pieces of art.

held in Maryland. In addition, he made the National Honor Society of High Schools and was listed in *Who's Who Among High School Students* for 1983 and 1984. He graduated from high school in the top 5 percent of his class and received the State of Maryland Scholastic Merit Award.

After graduating from high school, Nguu enrolled at the University of Maryland with full scholarship support. "And yet," Nguu says now with a little laugh, "I did not enroll in art. I enrolled in engineering. Why? I wanted to make money, and I thought that was the way to do it."

But the pull of art would not be so easily put aside, and after his freshman year, he switched to a program of art study, including commercial art and graphic design. "From Americans," Nguu explains, "I have learned the importance of doing work that you truly like to do."

Nguu is fully aware of how much support he has received in America. During his years before emancipation, he lived with two different foster families. Although he is now staying with his sister and her husband, he still visits both of his former foster families regularly and sends messages to both foster mothers and foster fathers on Mother's Day and Father's Day.

"Actually," says Nguu, "I was so close to one of my counselors in high school that I feel I have three mothers in America."

Nguu also understands that he has a responsibility to pay back in kind some of the support that has contributed to his progress and development in this country. Two nights each week he tutors an unaccompanied refugee high school boy in mathematics and contemporary social issues. He is president of the University of Maryland Vietnamese Students Association and president of the Maryland Athletic Organization of Vietnamese.

"I think it is important to have more communication between refugees who are without families, after they are emancipated," Nguu says, "and more support. I hope I can help with that in the future."

12 "Of Profound Humanitarian Concern"

T ODAY the world has more refugees than ever before in its history. The United Nations Commissioner for Refugees (UNHCR) estimates that in Asia, Africa, and Central and South America over 10 million people have currently fled from their homelands because of political, religious, or economic turmoil. Most of them are living in refugee camps, often under grim conditions.

Probably as many as two thousand unaccompanied children are presently in the refugee camps of Southeast Asia, and new escapees arrive every month. No one knows how many children and teenagers are living alone in the poorer, less well-organized refugee camps of Africa, Mexico, and other Latin American countries. They have fled from fighting, political tyranny, or hunger in their homelands, often with parents (particularly in Africa) who died before or after reaching the refugee camps.

Once the UNHCR has determined that a child in a refugee camp cannot safely be returned to the country he or she came from (only rarely is that possible), the child should be resettled in another country as quickly as possible. Resettlement of young refugees from

Guatemalan children in a Mexican refugee camp. Water is often in short supply.

Southeast Asia is going forward at a generally satisfactory pace, but as yet almost no consideration has been given to those in African and Latin American camps. They are existing there in dangerous, even life-threatening conditions.

Even with the most liberal immigration policy, the United States can take but a small percentage of the people worldwide who want to make this country their home. But children living alone in refugee camps are the most vulnerable of all hopeful immigrants, the most desperate for help. That fact alone should carry heavy weight in setting immigration policy that would give a reasonable number of them priority consideration for immigration to the United States, no matter where they are in the world.

The United States has a long history of humanitarian effort in bringing unaccompanied refugee children to this country for resettlement. During World War II hundreds of children who had lost their parents were brought from Europe to America. After World War II, almost five thousand children came to America from Poland, Czechoslovakia, Hungary, and Germany under a "displaced persons" program. From 1953 to 1956 many unaccompanied refugee children

An Ethiopian refugee camp in Sudan.

came from Communist bloc countries of Europe under special U.S. programs, including the Hungarian Refugee Program following the Russian invasion of Hungary in 1956.

Between January, 1961, and October, 1962, after Fidel Castro came to power in Cuba, over fourteen thousand unaccompanied children were quietly sent out of that country and brought into the United States in a remarkable and little-known program called Operation Pedro Pan (Peter Pan). The parents of those children were willing to give them up rather than let them fall under the indoctrination of Castro's Communist government.

In the forty-five years since World War II and especially since the end of the war in Vietnam, a number of fine organizations have acquired insights, expertise, and deep feeling in helping unaccompanied refugee youth build new lives in America. They stand ready to continue to provide that help. In shaping future immigration policy, the United States government should not forget the words of its own State Department and Immigration and Naturalization Service that unaccompanied refugee children are "a subject of profound humanitarian concern."

Bibliography

Books

Ashabranner, Brent. *Children of the Maya: A Guatemalan Indian Odyssey.*
New York: Dodd, Mead & Co., 1985.
————. *The New Americans: Changing Patterns in U.S. Immigration.*
New York: Dodd, Mead & Co., 1982.
Borton, Lady. *Sensing the Enemy.* Garden City, N.Y.: The Dial
Press, 1984.
Lawon, Don. *The United States in the Vietnam War.* New York:
Thomas Y. Crowell, 1981.
Lifton, Betty Jean and Thomas C. Fox. *Children of Vietnam.* New
York: Atheneum, 1972.
Mabie, C. J. *Vietnam: There and Here.* New York: Henry Holt &
Co., 1986.

Special Reports and Articles

In Our Fathers' Land: Vietnamese Amerasians in America by Sr. Marilyn
Lacey. The United States Catholic Conference. Washington,
D.C., 1985.
*Of Special Humanitarian Concern: U. S. Refugee Admissions Since Passage
of the Refugee Act* by Dennis Gallagher, Susan Forbes, and

Patricia Weiss Fagen. Refugee Policy Group. Washington,
    D.C., September, 1985.
"The Refugee Explosion" by Tad Szulc. *The New York Times Magazine*,
    November 23, 1980.
Toward Emancipation. Proceedings of unaccompanied refugee minors
    conference, San Diego, California, March 9–11, 1983, United
    States Catholic Conference, Lutheran Immigration and Ref-
    ugee Service, U.S. Office of Refugee Resettlement.
Unaccompanied Minor Refugees: Nine Years of Achievement. Proceedings
    of conference, Chevy Chase, Maryland, November 13–16,
    1984. Sponsors: Lutheran Immigration and Refugee Service,
    U.S. Office of Refugee Resettlement, United States Catholic
    Conference. Published by United States Catholic Conference,
    Washington, D.C., 1986.
*Unaccompanied Refugee Children: The Evolution of U.S. Policies—1939
    to 1984* by Susan S. Forbes and Patricia Weiss Fagen. Refugee
    Policy Group. Washington, D.C., August, 1984.
*Voyagers in the Land: A Report on Unaccompanied Southeast Asian Refugee
    Children*. United States Catholic Conference. Washington,
    D.C., 1983, revised 1984.

Index